The Burnings

Himanjali is an editor and writer. Her children's and YA books include *The Stupendous Timetelling Superdog* and *Talking of Muskaan*, which were shortlisted for the Crossword Book Awards. *Mrs C Remembers*, her first novel for adults, won her the FICCI Publishing Award for Upcoming Author of the Year in 2018. Her first picture book for children, *Forgetful Dida*, was published in April 2024.

Himanjali likes birthday cakes with candles, the rhythm of waves breaking on a shore, the first glimpse of mountain peaks on long car journeys, with a dog settled on her lap and a child's sleepy head on her shoulder.

The Burnings

HIMANJALI SANKAR

Here's to burning brighter!

Himanjali

2025.

PAN

First published 2025 by Pan
an imprint of Pan Macmillan Publishing India Private Limited
707 Kailash Building
26 K. G. Marg, New Delhi 110001
www.panmacmillan.co.in

Pan Macmillan, The Smithson, 6 Briset Street, Farringdon, London EC1M 5NR
Associated companies throughout the world
www.panmacmillan.com

ISBN 978-93-95624-74-9

This is a work of fiction. Names, characters, businesses, organizations, places, events, and incidents either are the product of the author's imagination or are used fictitiously. Any resemblance to actual persons, living or dead, events, or locales is entirely coincidental.

1 3 5 7 9 8 6 4 2

Typeset in Petersburg by R. Ajith Kumar, New Delhi
Printed and bound in India by Thomson Press India Ltd.

for ma and baba and their life stories, those I know and those I don't, that find their way into mine regardless.

And travellers, now, within that valley,
Through the red-litten windows see
Vast forms that move fantastically
To a discordant melody;
While, like a ghastly rapid river,
Through the pale door
A hideous throng rush out forever,
And laugh—but smile no more.

– EDGAR ALLAN POE, 'The Haunted Palace'

PROLOGUE
The Burnings

There was an ocean in the small room, deep slate-grey water undulating like a seesaw, curling and crashing into its four walls soundlessly. The petite woman with a caterpillar unibrow crawling across her forehead knew she would be thrown against one of the walls if she wasn't careful. The strong current forced her towards a dark, dank corner. The door was invisible, though it was seven feet tall, obscured by the rising, opaque water. She strained every muscle to tread water and stay in the middle of the ocean room. The waves slanted and surged until she had a hard time keeping her head above the surface. As they crested, she moved upwards sharply, dizzyingly, the top of her head almost touching the ceiling.

That's when she saw the spindly, lizard-like little girl. She was barely ten, but there were deep crescent shadows under her wide-set beady eyes. Her hair hung in limp, tangled strands, framing a face too pasty, almost translucent, as if the very life had been drained from her. Sitting in a tiny boat that was swaying madly, she painted large red and yellow flames onto the waves that rolled against the side of the boat. She dipped her paintbrush in the ocean every now and then, releasing blazing colours into the water in dizzying eddies.

The girl was at ease, unlike the terrified woman. She started singing, a shrill, nasal, tuneless 'Fire on the mountain, run, run, run!' A small lump of disfigured flesh in the shape of a little heart – pulsating, half-covered with glassy skin – protruded like a raw wound from her left collarbone. The girl stopped singing as suddenly as she had started and fingered the abscess with the sharp nail of her index finger until a pale yellow dot of pus oozed out. Their eyes met. The little girl smiled at the woman, with narrowed, still cold eyes. The woman couldn't smile back – her lips refused to oblige, they wouldn't curl upwards – but her unibrow bristled like a caterpillar in motion, a swollen wave on her forehead.

An old, familiar fear gripped the woman. She swam towards the door, wanting to get away, but the little girl followed along on her boat, still looking at her, smiling politely. And then, she turned away, the boat carrying her out of the door as it opened wide, rocking to and fro on its hinges.

The fire that had spread from the tip of the girl's brush seemed to vaporize. The ocean gushed out through the open door, leaving the cold marble floor bare and glistening. The wall of grey-blue water that formed outside the room blocked the woman's view of the girl. However, she *could* see a window at the other end of the little room now that the water had receded – more a small barred opening than a window, really. A woman sat erect on a high barstool next to it, in an old-fashioned grey nightgown with a high neckline and long, puffed sleeves.

The two women looked at each other – the woman in the nightgown whispered 'the burnings, the burnings', her lips shaping the words emphatically, though her voice struggled to come out. The petite woman was hollowed out with fear, breathless, unable to move even though the water was gone. Her hair, streaked through with purple, was drenched.

The women didn't know each other, except in their dreams and through the paintings on the walls of a room. Not this room on the edge of an illusion but another, in a crumbling mansion on a mountain. And the pale reptilian girl, they both knew her. These silken threads, though tenuous, formed a tight web, spreading and drawing them together.

The woman by the window didn't seem to care that the little girl had left the room, as if summoned by the looming night-coloured mansion in the mountains. But the purple-haired woman felt despair, cold and terrifying, coursing through her. If only she could move, go towards the odd little girl. The girl, with the throbbing, disfigured heart on her collarbone, who had started singing again. They couldn't see her but the shrill, nasal voice rang out as clearly as when she was in the room. 'Fire on the mountain, run, run run!'

1

the woman in the room

There were moments of lucidity. Hours altogether sometimes. Often, she spoke out loud. The nurse, in her starched white uniform, knee-high socks and polished black shoes like a schoolgirl, listened. The woman was grateful for that. After a lifetime of silence, even as her mind slipped away to god knows where, she was grateful for these moments of sharing; the nurse nodding, seemingly empathetic.

One day she remembered Justin, her first boyfriend. She had been only fifteen then. The perfect age for first love – innocent, deep, full of promises that were meant to be broken. His hands eagerly exploring under her clothes, her lips seeking his as her heart thudded at the excitement of it all.

The nurse laughed, scandalized. 'But when did you meet Sir?' She wanted to move the conversation to the ordered parameters of matrimony and legal belonging; it was disgusting to her that an old woman could talk about hands fumbling on her breasts.

But the woman didn't really want to talk about her husband. 'I met Avyukt Gupta at a fundraiser,' she said, her voice prim with misgiving, lips pursed.

The nurse nodded. Everyone in their small town knew of Avyukt Gupta's romance, how he had gone to London and returned with the beautiful Disha, who had charmed and shocked the townspeople.

She looked at her patient, clad in an unfashionable grey nightgown, and found that it was surprisingly easy to imagine a younger version of the woman in strappy dresses that her mother-in-law would have disapproved of.

'Avyukt Gupta – polished, suave, one of those boarding school boys who never get over the perfection of their childhoods,' the woman said with a snigger. But she was speaking with hindsight. She hadn't found him a stereotype all those years back – thirty-five or forty it must have been? Just a handsome and pleasant young man, working for the already successful family business while his younger brother struggled under his exemplary shadow.

The woman remembered more than she cared to share. She had been swept off her feet by Avyukt Gupta's courtship. The early days were good but those memories felt contrived now, compromised by the bitterness of the later years. How could they stay pristine after all that had happened? And then, as always, her mind started slipping, like the fog that descended on the mountainous slopes outside her mansion, obscuring the landscape, burying it, until for all purposes it didn't matter what lay beneath.

The days ahead were bound to be brittle, confused. The woman knew that. Time was not on her side. If she wanted to have her way, she would have to act quickly.

The nurse sighed. She knew her patient. When the woman's mind left the room and her stories turned to gibberish, the nurse played along. 'You know, after that, it happened … you know, something that … do you get it?' The woman would look confused, making no sense, even to herself. She could no longer remember what she had said just five minutes ago. On some days the nurse enjoyed troubling her, asking teasing counter-questions that bewildered the woman till she fell silent. Inevitably, her mind wiped clean, she would sit silently in the room, rocking back and forth, as the nurse went back to her cross-stitch, laughing to herself and shaking her head regretfully. The ways of the wealthy and corrupt. She had seen it all, she could tell you a thing or two.

the woman who left

The fire was enormous – it had consumed everything in its way, effortlessly and completely. The rooms, the house, the garden – all of it now a formless mass of red flames and ashes; shaking, agitated. When there was nothing left for the fire to eat, it slowed down; languorous little tongues in the dark, millions of them, probing, licking the crevices of a million moist mouths. And in the corner of the nothingness that it had reduced everything to stood the little girl with limp, tangled hair and bruise-like shadows under soulless eyes. The fleshy, heart-shaped growth on her left collarbone pulsated as she stood with a smile on her thin, colourless lips, her body slithering against the low boundary wall of the garden as if she was moving to a discordant tune that only she could hear.

Vasundhara was sitting upright on her bed, trying to unsee the little girl who still, after all these years, had the power to undo her like nothing else. She tried to reason with herself that it was the fault of the fires that were making headlines these days – strange, inexplicable fires that were breaking out all over the world, perplexing the best scientific minds and triggering her worst memories.

She shut her mind down, summoning a blank state of nothingness where her thoughts used to be, from which she would emerge when she was ready, unaware of how much time had lapsed but poised to live again. She'd learnt how to do that, as neatly as shutting a book without putting in a bookmark. She would lose the page and not return to that chapter. Not until her mind insisted, forced her to revisit the nightmares stacked inside her like Russian dolls, one opening up and leading to the next, leaving her breathless and screaming 'Fire!' in the middle of the night.

Vasundhara had found it hard to love the girl. The girl who refused to breastfeed, who screamed while being bathed, who spat out her food and only loved her father. The girl who stared at her mother with cold disdain. She, in turn, reconciled herself to it.

'Why are you looking at me like that?' Vasundhara had lightly asked her one day when she was three.

'Because I hate you.' The little girl had said it clearly yet with the enunciation of a child. Apropos of nothing. It was not a childish 'I hate you' in light of thwarted plans. Just a straightforward hatred that had stayed constant from the day she was born.

'Don't say that to your mother,' the dad had reprimanded. Vasundhara had shaken her head as if it didn't matter. But of course it did. When the newborn was placed in her arms for the first time, Vasundhara had been filled with an odd sense of trepidation. A lizard-shaped baby in her arms. She had instantly wanted to fling it away. Though that moment passed she could never shake it off, her aversion to the spindly, chalky baby with beady eyes. Sometimes she wondered if things would have been different if she had loved the baby the moment it was placed in her arms – perhaps then she wouldn't have grown into the little girl that she did. It was what mothers were meant to do: fall in love with their newborn babies, not feel the urge to throw them away.

All of that was in the past, though it could still bite. It hadn't lost its claws and it found insidious ways into her life when she was least expecting it. It was true that Vasundhara had a history with unaccountable fires, but it was ridiculous to think even for a moment that such a global event was linked to her own little life. She tried to laugh at how ludicrous the idea was as her mind kept returning to the child that had wriggled and darted like a lizard on a wall in her sleep, clicking her tongue and pushing it in and out of her mouth in quick movements.

Vasundhara felt that familiar anticipatory fear of what was to come settling on her after all these years, like an old friend reclaiming a space best left empty. It would always be this way. The past would catch up when she thought she had left it behind. Her mind would sink, rendering her breathless with fear. She wished it could be otherwise. But it wasn't possible, not for her. Not after everything that had happened with the little girl who hated her mother and kindled quivering fires that consumed whatever displeased her.

the woman who was unafraid of fire

I knew I would go. I had reached that point of calm one inevitably does after a long period of loving someone more than one should. When you are able to fold away the love, smooth its edges, make a neat square of it and tuck it away in the lowest depths of your chest of drawers. I could think of Akshar as if he was just a friend now; I could talk to him on the phone without my heart lighting up, or WhatsApp him a thought and not check my phone endlessly till he replied. Sometimes it still hurt a little but it was a breezy, almost pleasurable, pain. Like today when I saw a black- and brown-spotted stray dog who looked just like Jugaad – even in the way he was trotting briskly as if on an important mission, head held high, tail slightly raised.

The fire in the gatekeeper's cottage in school fifteen years ago, when Akshar's little brother was visiting. The charred remains of Jugaad's tiny doggy body. I had to stop and try to breathe as I searched for my inhaler in my handbag.

When I came home, I saw the email. I must have missed it in the hustle of office and impossible deadlines. I didn't open it right away. I ate my takeaway noodles and honey chicken, bathed and settled down on the bed as I did every night. And then I started reading.

Akshar never used words that let on – one had to search through the alphabets, disassemble and then assemble them again to understand. Which was why this email surprised me. It was naked in its desire. Come this weekend, please. Just for a few days. I am dying. Almost immediately, I called him from my phone. He picked up just as I was about to hang up.

'Yes,' he said, as if I'd asked a question and that was his answer, as if we still spoke to each other every day as we used to. 'Have you had dinner?'

'Yes,' I mirrored. 'What happened?'

'Will you come?' he asked after a long silence, long enough that I had begun to think he would apologize for the email, say he was in a stupid mood when he wrote it and that I should forget about it. 'Will you?'

I didn't need this, and I owed him nothing. I had work deadlines.

Then there were the fires that headlined every news portal these days, every social media post. Fires that seemed to spring out of nowhere on tarred roads and highways, springing up walls of heat and light that made no sense. I hadn't seen one yet, no one I knew had, but we had all heard of the people who had walked into these fires and died. Or those who had gone close enough to inhale the fumes and fall sick but resisted the pull of the flames. And finally, those that had just turned away from the raging infernos, indifferent. It sounded crazy – I had refused to believe the stories when they first started coming in from the US, like most others. But three months had passed, and too many stories surrounded us. One couldn't ignore them anymore.

A few mysterious fires had been reported in India, too, now. They had been written about in detail, discussed, dissected for days and at length. The first recorded case involved a fourteen-year-old schoolboy – athletic, popular, with spiky hair and deep dimples. He had just walked towards the fire – briskly, purposefully – and stood there, smiling, in the midst of the translucent yellow–orange–red that consumed him. He, in turn, seemed to swallow the light as the fire disappeared, leaving his body broken, blackened, inflamed. The bystanders who called the ambulance said he was muttering something, his face all swollen and disfigured. On reaching the hospital he was declared dead.

The next couple of cases were fatal as well: an autorickshaw driver who sped into a fire that sprung up right in front of him, a woman who put down a bag of vegetables she was carrying before walking into the fire, slowly. But there had been stories of those who survived, too. A pregnant woman in her early thirties who was now in the hospital with minor burns. Doctors had confirmed that the foetus seemed unharmed. A seventy-two-year-old man and his wife also came away unscathed, after she pulled him back and the six-feet-high fire died right there, an inch away from them. A middle-aged failed entrepreneur from a small town in Karnataka was still in the ICU, unconscious but reportedly stable.

Globally, the numbers were already staggering. Lockdowns were being announced, people had been advised to stay off the roads and indoors. So much uncertainty, so much chaos, it was definitely not the time to plan a sudden trip – driving up hilly roads would be foolhardy.

'I can come but just, you know … everything is crazy. It's not a good time to travel,' I said to Akshar, though some part of me already knew I couldn't say no to him.

'Are you scared of the fires?' Akshar asked, mockingly it seemed. Ironic coming from someone who had sent me a dramatic 'I am dying' email. Come to think of it, what kind of person would send such an email? But Akshar was Akshar.

'No, but flights are being cancelled …'

'You can take the train. The overnight train is never crowded. I'll send my driver to the station to pick you up. There's not been a single instance of fire on the roads in our area.'

Akshar had described the car journey to his home so many times, often on the last day of school when our bags were packed and everyone was leaving. The air getting cooler and cooler as one left the railway station behind, as the car wound up and around hairpin bends that made one's stomach clench. Akshar was always elated for days before the school holidays, looking forward so much to being with his family and friends, to return to his mansion in the hills. It used to make me jealous, his happiness at our parting, his yearning for the mountains he loved best. Though primarily I was jealous because I knew the biggest reason why he was so eager to go home. He didn't always say it, but I knew. It was obvious.

'I need to be in the office for the rest of this week, but I can leave on Saturday,' I said to Akshar now, scrolling through the calendar on my laptop.

'If you catch the evening train, you'll arrive at the station at 6 a.m. Jai Singh will bring you here, well in time for lunch on Sunday afternoon.' Akshar's voice, usually light and measured, was almost shrill with excitement. I felt a twinge of unease.

'I'll stay for four days or so, okay?' I said. 'I will need to get back to work soon, and, you know ...'

'Cool, wonderful. I'll book your tickets right away, and email them to you.'

'Oh, don't be silly. I'll do the booking. Don't worry.'

'No, no,' Akshar insisted. 'I invited you. You are my guest. I'll send you the tickets.'

Before I could reply, he hung up. Sixteen minutes later, my tickets were in my inbox. All of a sudden, I was seeing Akshar in five days. The last time we had met was five *years* ago at our school reunion. He no longer let me know when he was coming down to Delhi. Earlier, we would meet for a meal or drinks; he would never come here for more than one night.

'I can't stay away from home for too long,' Akshar would say, drumming his long fingers on the table impatiently. I had no idea why he couldn't. He lived the life of a feudal lord in his ancestral mansion, high in the Himalayas. What did feudal lords have to do except lead debauched lives and occasionally rise to magnanimously meet the desperate pleas of suffering villagers?

'I thought you had a well-oiled machinery up there. Surely you can afford to be away now and then?' I had once allowed myself to ask.

'I suppose,' he had said, the faraway look in his grey-green eyes telling me that he had only half-listened to my question. It frustrated me, that look. It always had. Even when we were kids and best friends, and later, when we were teenagers and in love.

My first love. Not his, though. His first love had always been Aahana. The girl in the hills who shared his birthday. He spoke about his friend in his hometown all the time when we were children, when we first came to boarding school. Our brief teenage romance didn't hold a chance against the light of his eternal love for Aahana.

Aahana meant immortal and so did Akshar – he had also told me that. Both names were chosen by his father: one for his son and one for the Navy man next door's daughter. A favour bestowed by the imperial master on a grateful subject perhaps, honouring the fortuitous coincidence that the two children had been born on the same day.

Akshar's tightly controlled sense of self had never allowed him to ask for help from anyone. Neither did mine but I had never had anyone slavishly doting on me either. He knew when it came to me, he only had to ask. And how could I ever say no to Akshar?

The next day, I went into Mukul's very messy cubicle, with papers strewn across his desk and books stacked against the wall, spines misaligned. I cradled my cup of black coffee and said, 'I'm taking off for the hills for a few days, at the end of this week.'

If Mukul was surprised, he didn't let on. 'Just?' he asked. We had only been together for a few months. We were careful about boundaries, about not overstepping.

'You remember my friend Akshar?' I asked. Mukul nodded. 'I received a strange email from him yesterday. He said he wants me to visit because he is dying.'

It struck me for the first time, as I said this aloud, how awful it was. Mukul raised his eyebrows. 'Oh wow, of course. I mean, you must go. What happened?'

'I called and asked, but he didn't say. So I thought I'll just go, stay with him for a few days and return by mid next week.'

It sounded neat when I put it like that. Sensible and obvious. A friend had reached out in desperation, and I would have to go.

'Not sure you should be travelling right now, with the fires spouting everywhere, but if your friend is … I guess.' Fires were not spouting everywhere, I wanted to point out, though they sounded horrifying and senseless, driving the whole world insane.

'I feel I have to go, Mukul. It'll just be a few days.' It pleased me, I must admit, that he didn't seem to want me to leave.

'I was going to ask if you want to stay at mine for a few days, but if you are leaving on the weekend …'

I did like the idea. Of staying with Mukul, moving in with him even. I felt my habitual reserve slipping.

'When I return on Thursday, I could come to yours?' I asked. I felt embarrassed at how eager I sounded and quickly added, 'For a few days, of course.'

'I would like that,' he said, his voice so deep and warm that I felt like going home with him right away.

'And there's three days before I leave …'

'Yes,' he smiled. I smiled back rather foolishly.

The rest of the day went by in a whirl of meetings and training sessions. We were being taught how to operate without the office LAN so we wouldn't be required to come in for the next couple of weeks at least. As a graphic designer I just needed the client briefs; my job wasn't people-facing as such. I liked the idea of working from home, but it felt surreal to suddenly change our work patterns and lifestyles with no real idea as to why we were getting ready on a war footing. What had brought on these fires? Speculation was rife. Biological warfare, environmental disaster, even divine retribution. Was there a terrorist mastermind behind them, or some political intrigue on an unprecedented scale?

After prolonged goodbyes and hugs with colleagues who were friends, Mukul and I left work at 6 p.m.

'See you,' said Rhea, the receptionist, with a shake of her head. The plan was for everyone to work from home as much as possible to minimize the risk of harm. Apparently three or four fires had broken out in Delhi that day itself. We didn't have the details yet, but the situation was worsening for sure.

'Sooner rather than later, I hope,' I babbled. 'Take care, be safe.'

Mukul looked at me quizzically as we walked down the corridor. 'Are you okay?'

'Yeah, I guess. All this fire shit is confusing me.'

'Yes, baba, I know. I'm worried about you travelling in the middle of all this.'

Mukul had been going on about the fires for the last week, theorizing that climate change was manifesting in ways hitherto unknown, including the outbreak of fires. He seemed to think the world was on the verge of ending.

'I don't know – it's just all so overblown and alarmist,' I started. Except it was all getting so serious, and I didn't know what to think anymore.

We shared a bottle of wine on Mukul's terrace. The narrow road that the balcony overlooked was deserted. He wanted me to stay the night but I longed for my own bed, my red tartan bedsheet and fluffy pillows. To spend some time on my own after a long, confusing day. To prepare myself for the hills, pack a bag.

'It's only Wednesday – you have three days before you leave.' Mukul sounded a little exasperated.

'Then you come and stay with me. Tomorrow?'

'I'll come day after,' he said. 'And drop you at the station on Saturday, okay? Tomorrow I've promised to have dinner with my parents.'

'Okay,' I said, kissing him. 'Yes. See you Friday.'

I couldn't sleep that night. Not properly. A series of strange dreams fitfully collapsed into each other. In one of them I was in Mukul's car and almost at the railway station when he suddenly changed his mind about dropping me off and kept driving around and around the outer circle of Connaught Place. I woke up sweating, thinking of Akshar, worrying about how I would get to him.

The next morning the news wasn't good. Many flights were being cancelled because two fires had broken out at airports in Chennai and Jaipur. The Jaipur airport reported a couple of hospitalizations though none of them were serious – minor burns and trauma, expected to be back home in a day. There had been one casualty in the Chennai fire – a member of the runway staff. His co-worker who had witnessed the incident was terrified, and his statement to the press had left everyone on edge.

'He was just walking, towards the fire … straight,' the man had said stutteringly, his face ashen, eyes bulging. 'And then … and then … he turned around, he smiled at me. I didn't know, I didn't realize, I didn't try to stop him. He … he just walked into the fire as if he was entering a room through an open door. Just like that, he was gone.' The man had broken down sobbing. The newsclip had gone viral. It was all that everyone, everywhere, was watching.

My first instinct was to check if trains were running as per schedule. Thankfully, they were. I wished I'd planned to leave earlier, but I hadn't expected the office to declare work-from-home from Wednesday itself. There was still a lot of work to finish, though. I would carry my laptop to the hills but didn't plan to work for the few days I would be there if I could help it.

In the afternoon I got a text from Akshar: Please don't cancel your trip. I need you.

I felt my heart tighten. How many years had it been since I'd heard such words from Akshar? I tried not to wonder why they still mattered. After all these years, all that happened in the interim, I was back in boarding school, sitting on a rock in the school playground, with Jugaad licking my feet and Akshar, his face dappled with sunlight, saying, 'I need you so much, you know that, Shalini, you've always known that, haven't you?'

'I have,' I had said, straightening my tie as I got up. It was ridiculous that we had to wear a tie every day. 'You need me, and so does Jugaad.'

Jugaad, devoted to Akshar and me, wagged his tail dutifully when he heard me say his name. It was the way he carried himself that I loved the most – like a busy canine ballerina on his tiptoes, always ready to break into a pirouette.

'Yes, we are a family – you, me and Jugaad,' Akshar had said. 'He is the dad, I'm the mom and you are our child.'

'Very funny, Akshar,' I had said, as we started walking towards the school building in the evening sun. Jugaad danced between us. 'I want to be the parent, you be the child.'

There had been something so calm and peaceful about Akshar that evening. He hadn't been filled with restless energy, pacing up and down, loving and fidgety at the same time in his peculiar way. I had always known a part of him yearned for Aahana. The one for whom he could give his life, he had once said, unexaggerated and serious. That evening, though, it had seemed I was enough. And now, some fifteen years later, I still cherished it; that rare feeling of Akshar being only mine, even if just for a few hours.

2

the woman in the room

On some days the woman just sat quietly and swept out the unaired corners of her mind before they darkened and disappeared again. It was at these moments that she thought of her parents in London. Did they know she wasn't alright? Locked up in a dingy room with barred windows and left to rot. Why didn't they come and take her away? To her childhood, to London, to manicured lawns and parks. Then she could just visit India in her dreams like she used to as a child, after long summer holidays spent with grandparents, cousins and aunts and uncles.

At times she wondered about her cousins, Roon and Bulbul. The three of them had formed a club one summer, the Clickers, when they were seven or eight years old. It was secret and exclusive – membership required these empty boxes of chewing gum that made a clicking sound when they were shut. Not gum perhaps, some form of fancy imported mint, not easily available in India back then. She must have brought them from London for her favourite cousins. They had spent hours writing a secret anthem which started with 'We are the clickers, click click click'. The other cousins bent over backwards to be invited to join this club. They wanted that coveted little plastic box to join in singing the anthem. It was pretty much a preparation for adult life, for exclusion, for elitist rules that kept people out.

Avyukt and she were social people, a charming couple, always invited, always included. As their marriage crumbled, so did the rest. But all that was later. At first, there were the interminable parties, here, there, everywhere. In London, Bombay, Delhi. You needed a certain kind of energy for it; they couldn't make it last like many of their friends did. Besides, Avyukt was besotted with his secret girlfriend, who he thought no one knew about. It was quite sweet in its own way if she thought about it clinically. A love that grew against all barriers, helplessly.

The other day when the doctor had come to see her, she had said, 'We are the clickers, click click click.' It was the wrong thing to say. The doctor had smiled and asked, 'What?' Her tongue had got thick, her mind clouded and she couldn't remember anymore. She had seen the doctor and the nurse exchanging glances. The nurse had sighed, 'She just says these words … no meaning.'

She had wanted to explain. There *was* meaning. Just because the nurse didn't understand didn't make it senseless.

Here she was, at the mercy of these inane people, no freedom, not allowed to be in touch with the outside world – how could her mind help but shrink to the size of the room in which she was confined? She would tell her dad to take her away. Her dad was a powerful figure in London. More important than Avyukt Gupta, who she never should have married. He was the one keeping her locked up, telling people she was going mad, so he could be with that other woman whose name she could no longer remember. That stupid other woman, as stupid as her husband.

'It's not like I never took lovers. After I got married, that is,' she had said aloud instead. It wasn't only Avyukt who had cheated; that pleasure wasn't his alone. The nurse had cupped her hands over her mouth. Idiotic pleb. The doctor had shaken his head, his expression solemn. There was a third person in the room whom she couldn't recognize. Was it Avyukt? Whoever he was, he had angrily exclaimed, 'Unbelievable!' and stormed out of the room. Good riddance. She didn't have time for these prudes. These fake doctors and carers. They should just leave her alone. She wasn't useless like them. She had important things to do.

the woman who left

That night Vasundhara didn't dream of fire, but the little girl was there again. In the T-shirt with a big sunflower on it, as always. Her hair fell to her shoulders, as lifeless as she looked. The dark circles under her eyes were bluish-black, wounded half-moons, and on her hands were coarse, bluish-

black woollen mittens. On a closer look, though, they weren't mittens after all – it was her fingers, melted into a lump of charred, rounded flesh.

The girl couldn't use her burnt, mutilated hands. But she didn't appear to care as she ran around the driveway, kicking a ball until it went through the windshield of an old, nondescript Swift Dzire parked there. The glass didn't shatter – the ball passed through it as if it was air. Vasundhara saw a man slumped over the steering wheel. The little girl slithered and wriggled against the phantom windshield, bringing her face close to his head. Her glassy eyes glistened as she smiled and nodded to herself, her tongue flickering in and out of her mouth, licking her paper-dry lips greedily.

Vasundhara managed to stifle her scream, as she got up with a start. She sat ramrod straight, her heart hammering so intensely that it was painful. She wanted to go back into the dream so badly, to check if the man at the wheel was still alive, if he still thought of her. If he still loved her, even a little. She was crying now. Tears were streaming down her cheeks. But it wasn't the dream that had made her cry. It was the man. Adil. The man for whom she had left her husband twenty-five years ago. And who had left her because of her little girl – the spooky little girl who refused to love.

She went to the kitchen and took big, thirsty gulps of water till her throat stopped hurting.

It wasn't that Vasundhara wished she had done anything differently. She didn't wish she hadn't walked out of her marriage, nor did she wish she had sacrificed her own happiness for that of others. Perhaps some people did such things successfully but she was sure she never could. She didn't like the word *sacrifice.* Apart from everything else it reminded her of fire – sacrificial fires that claimed to purify. Such hypocrisy, such rubbish.

In her weakest moments she still craved Adil. But what could Vasundhara have done? Adil refused to return to her as long as the girl was there, and where would she have gone? The little girl who had learnt how to light matches before she knew how to walk – who had stared at her mother venomously when Vasundhara entered the room, and screamed and thrown away the match with its still-burning tip. How had the spindly baby, who could only crawl, got hold of a matchbox?

Vasundhara did have a few brief years of happiness with Adil when the child lived with her father but then the little girl had come to stay with them, and things became worse than ever before.

the woman who was unafraid of fire

When Mukul came over on Friday, he reiterated that he wasn't happy about me going to visit Akshar. I could recall a drunken evening almost a year ago, when we were just friends – I had cried on his shoulder about how I would always be hung up on Akshar, my childhood love. I had no idea if Mukul remembered that.

'I mean, who writes "I am dying", like literally, when asking a friend to visit? It's just not normal,' he said, using air quotes and rolling his eyes.

'I think I know the difference between saying something like "I am dying to see you" and "I am dying and need you, my friend, to visit." In any case, when did I ever say Akshar is normal?' And then because it was all so macabre and funny I laughed, though Mukul only frowned. I didn't quite buy into it either – Akshar couldn't die while I continued to live. It wasn't possible.

'Also, the fires. They make me worried. This is not the time for travel.'

I didn't comment that this was the fifth time in one hour he had said this. 'The frequency is so low in India that we don't even know a single person – I mean personally – who has seen a fire. I know it's happening but it's under control as of now.'

Mukul, unlike me, didn't hesitate to point out that I was repeating myself. 'Which is why we have to be careful. How many times will you say the frequency is low, as if we must wait for the situation to get out of control to start taking precautions?'

His reasoning was solid, I had to admit. Curfews were being declared every other day in regions that had witnessed multiple fires, as if to placate the wrath of nature. It would be a long drive up to Akshar's house – forget about fire, if there was a curfew would cars be allowed on the streets? Earlier that day, I had called Akshar to ask if we should cancel or postpone but he had said rather highhandedly that his car would never be stopped by anyone, so fuck the curfews.

'Who does he think he is?' asked Mukul when I told him this.

'They are these big shot feudal landlords – most of the area belongs to his family. The police don't mess with them.'

'Wow!' he said sarcastically. 'And you like the idea of these marauding, law-breaking landlords?'

'I've known Akshar since I was seven. I don't judge him by his family.' I tried to keep my voice level, though I was getting all mad inside.

By the time we arrived at the railway station on Saturday night, we were mellow and loving, softened by the idea of being apart for some days in these uncertain times. Mukul bought me chocolates on the platform; I hugged him and wished we hadn't been so on edge with each other over the last few days. 'I'll be back soon. I'll miss you.'

The second AC coach, with its cave-like interiors, blue berths and long, darkened windows, made me nostalgic for all the train journeys of my life, and I suddenly wished Mukul was coming with me. I couldn't remember the last time I'd travelled by train – maybe five or six years ago – but it still felt so achingly familiar. I loved the cold, and the scratchy blankets and starched white sheets the attendant would hand out soon. It was the routine of childhood. I wanted to tell Mukul all about it. But he was already looking at his watch. It was time for him to deboard.

'See you on the 25th?' I asked.

'Yes, I'll be here,' Mukul said. 'Call and message, okay?'

'I will,' I nodded, adding, 'It's only four days anyway.'

'Right. Shalini. Bye.' He said the three words separately, with pauses in between that sounded odd but somehow nice. 'See you very soon then.'

With that, Mukul was off. My mind had been racing for the past few days – my thoughts disordered and confused, about Akshar, about Mukul, about everything really – but now I just felt exhausted. I climbed into the upper berth and before I knew it, I was fast asleep, rocking like a baby to the rhythm of the speeding train. I slept fitfully though, waking up repeatedly to check the time despite having set my alarm for 5:45 a.m. and asked the attendant to wake me up in time for my stop.

It was pitch dark when I got off the train. The air was crisp and cold. Akshar's driver, Jai Singh, was waiting at the platform. With his bristling moustache and cropped hair, he could have been in the military. I asked him when he'd arrived and whether there was a curfew in the hills that day.

'Yes, madam. A small fire broke out a couple days ago on the road near this railway station. One woman had to be hospitalized, but there were no deaths,' he said. 'And today of course, the prime minister has called for a nationwide curfew, which everyone will have to follow.'

'But not us? We won't reach before noon, will we?'

Jai Singh gave me a disapproving glance, as if it was all my fault. Which I suppose it was – he wouldn't have had to disobey the prime minister if I hadn't come. 'No one will stop us,' he said flatly.

'But the prime minister's special forces – if any member of them sees us there will be trouble, right?' I asked anxiously. I mean, well-connected Akshar was but the Special Squad was notorious. I had no idea what sort of presence they had in the hills. Perhaps it was better there than in the city. Jai Singh simply strode ahead as if I'd not spoken. He opened the door of a black XUV – the only car parked outside the entrance of the station.

I asked him if we could keep the windows down. I could already smell the distant pines, but there was an almost burnt, toasty scent in the air as well. Or was I imagining it? As we left the station behind, I saw large dark triangles – like a child's drawing of mountains – etched in the distance. The sun hadn't risen yet. I leaned back and stared out of the window.

Children in boarding schools talk about their homes a lot. Describe them in detail to their friends as an act of remembering. Akshar was no exception. I could already imagine the black stone mansion with creepers on its walls and large windows, set firmly in one of those looming triangles. Ten bedrooms, a study and library, a banquet hall (yes, really, a banquet hall, as we weren't in the twenty-first century), a large family room with a projector and blank wall for watching movies, a grand living room with a fireplace for entertaining guests.

Akshar lived alone now in this large, formidable mansion. Over the last few years the family tree had withered, each branch breaking, falling off, till only he and his brother were left. As far as I knew, his brother

– ten years younger than us – was studying in the UK. His father had died ten years ago, and his mother more recently, though I didn't know exactly when.

I had texted Akshar a few months back as I occasionally did. I'd never minded being the one who, nine times out of ten, initiated any conversation between us but over time, my need to be in touch had lessened. At the reunion where we had last met, he had told me his mother wasn't keeping well. Akshar had always despised her. But a friend's mother had passed away around that time and I'd found myself thinking of Akshar. I had texted: How's your mom doing? His reply was: Oh she's gone. Even though I was used to Akshar's oddities, I was stunned by that. He hadn't even informed me. I put my phone down, reminded myself how much he hated her before writing, I am so very sorry Akshar.

Still, I wasn't ready for his callous reply, so completely devoid of sorrow. Good riddance.

To change the subject and cover my own sense of discomfort, I had asked him about Aahana. In the past many years, he had been evasive when it came to her. But that day he told me she had married a local doctor, who they had known since childhood and who had returned to their hometown as a general physician after studying abroad. I wondered, as the car wound its way uphill, if I would get to meet Aahana and her husband. Something had changed between them around the time Akshar's dad had died. Akshar had later said that Aahana and he would always remain friends, but there was nothing romantic left in their relationship. That his mother had won after all.

I had spent my life till then envying Aahana, wishing they would fall out of love. But when Akshar said there was nothing romantic between them anymore, I couldn't rejoice. I had always expected, someday, a call from Akshar telling me they were engaged to be married. I had prepared for that and strangely, I felt the announcement of an impending wedding wouldn't have sounded as horrid and dismal as Akshar saying the romance was gone. I knew immediately and with certainty that in the act of going away, the romance had eternalized itself; it had soaked into Akshar's very being and would never, ever leave him alone.

As the car wound its way up, one hairpin bend after another, my childhood carsickness resurfaced. Jai Singh was speeding in a way I was sure he would not have if Akshar was in the car. BETTER TO BE LATE, MR MOTORIST, THAN THE LATE MR MOTORIST read a corny cautionary hoarding at one nasty bend, which I wished Jai Singh would heed.

My stomach and mind were both churning, somewhat harmoniously – anxieties, memories, hopes and the tea I drank at the railway station all jostling against each other till I felt so squeamish that I asked Jai Singh to stop. He braked so hard that I had to rush out of the car as the bile rose in my throat. After vomiting my guts out, I felt better.

There was a burnt, leafless pine tree right next to me – spindly, slimy and reptilian in appearance, which sent a chill down my spine. Had there been a fire here? But Jai Singh said the fire had happened near the station; he hadn't mentioned one on the hills. Were there fires going unrecorded?

I picked up a pinecone that lay on the side of the road before returning to the car. There was something amazing about pinecones and how perfectly they were constructed, as if on a hilly assembly line run by invisible spirits that lived in all the quiet places. But now that I looked closely, this one was a bit grotesque – half-burnt, threatening to crumble in my hands. I threw it out of the window, repulsed, remembering the twisted, eerie tree it had come from. I fumbled for my inhaler and took a slow, deep breath.

'How much longer?' I asked. The infamous question that all children on long car journeys ask to drive their parents crazy.

'Still a long way,' Jai Singh said with the stoicism of a long-enduring parent, minus the love. 'You should try to sleep.'

I wished I had carried Avomine with me. Without medicine I wouldn't fall asleep, I knew.

It seemed to go on forever, all those relentless twists and turns that made my stomach clench and unclench. But just when I felt I couldn't bear it any longer, I found we were in front of an imposing iron gate with some sort of family crest monogrammed on it. The driveway stretched out, long and winding, behind the gate and all I could see were huge brooding trees on either side of the road, no sign of a house or mansion.

The guard stepped out of his box beside the gate and saluted. I sat up straight, smiled and nodded, unsure how one acknowledged saluting uniformed guards. The gates opened inwards, driven by some automation which made it rather eerie – the silent opening of unmanned gates. I leaned out of the window eagerly, relieved that the journey was almost over. I could see the top of a stone building and four turrets in the distance now. There seemed to be a solitary woman standing in one of the turrets, like a locked-up princess in a fairytale, but as the car took the next bend I lost sight of her. When I saw the building again it stretched, empty and vast, into the sky. There was a bird soaring above the precincts; maybe it had given the illusion of a lonely figure from this distance.

As Jai Singh turned the last corner and slowed down, a sense of inexplicable gloom made my heart sink. Faced with Akshar's imposing house, with its vacant eye-like windows and walls that were dull and lustreless like the skin of a terminally ill patient, I felt an iciness in my very bones which had nothing to do with the high altitude. I thought I caught a whiff of a burning smell in the air again. It had happened too many times in the last few hours. It was likely that I was imagining it.

A middle-aged man was coming down the flight of marble stairs that led up to the front door. They stretched wide, held up by fluted columns but with no banisters.

'Good afternoon, madam,' he said, eyes not meeting mine. He picked up my small purple suitcase and started climbing the stairs to the arched entrance. 'Myself Ravinder. Follow me.'

Jai Singh restarted the car and as he drove away to the garages I had seen on my way up, I wondered what I would do if he refused to take me down to the railway station on 25th March. It was a random thought which I shook off as best I could but when I went into the house, my sense of unease only intensified. It was dark inside – with moulded ceilings; dusty, faded thangkas mounted at regular intervals on the walls; the ebony blackness of the floors and the general air of grandeur and neglect.

We went up another flight of stairs. On the landing that branched into two flights of staircases I met a man with a stethoscope around his neck and a look of strange cunning in his pale eyes, wide-set and moist. He could have been good-looking if it weren't for those eyes. I wondered if this was Aahana's doctor husband. He must have come to see Akshar – a professional visit, going by the stethoscope and briefcase in his hand.

'Doctor *saab*,' Ravinder nodded without stopping and I followed him, throwing glances over my shoulder at 'Doctor saab', who smiled. The smile didn't reach his eyes.

On the next floor Ravinder went halfway down yet another dimly lit corridor before turning towards me and throwing open the door in front of him, ushering me into the presence of his master.

The room in which I found myself was large and lofty with long, narrow, pointed windows set at such a height from the wooden floors that it would be difficult for anyone but a giant to look out of them. Feeble, protracted gleams of sunlight lit up the room rather haphazardly – most of it, including the vaulted ceiling, remained in darkness. Heavy draperies shrouded most of the furniture except for one sofa with faded floral designs, on which Akshar was lying down. He rose when he saw me and came forward quickly to engulf me in a hug. He smelled clean and fresh, and I clung to that hug like a lifeline.

It took a few moments for me to register how altered his appearance was. His eyes were feverish, his cheeks hollow, the hair that fell long and straight to his shoulders was limp and greasy. There was an air of forced gaiety about him as he greeted me with questions that didn't really need answers. 'Was your journey comfortable, Shalini? You must have felt carsick? Jai Singh was waiting for you, right?'

He stopped to direct Ravinder, who was still standing near the door, to put my suitcase in the room that had been readied for me and to send in tea and snacks for us. We sat down at two ends of the long sofa and for a few minutes neither of us spoke – we just looked at each other and smiled. I didn't want Akshar to speak, to tell me anything. His face had always been remarkable. The aquiline, regal nose. His lips thin and pale but surpassingly beautiful in the way they curved upwards in a smile. I could go on.

'Akshar, why are you so pretty?' I asked. It was my favourite rhetorical ice-breaker with him.

'You know the answer, Shalini.' He was laughing.

'Yes, yes,' I sighed. 'Someone needs to be pretty enough for the two of us.'

'But you look ... wait ...' Akshar leaned back and scrunched his face in mock concern. 'Shalini, you are glowing. You look quite amazing. What the hell have you been up to?'

'Never mind that. Here we are again. You and me. Tell me what's going on, Akshar.'

'Always so impatient. All in good time. Can't you wait, Shalini?' The smile on his face softened his words.

'I can. We have four days. No hurries,' I replied. And I meant it. I wasn't in a hurry. I wanted to settle down, to enjoy the hills, to push aside the thoughts that jarred and focus on the ones that were calming. And then I would talk to Akshar. A long, long chat to understand what indeed was the matter. Why had he summoned me in this way? It didn't seem as though he was dying. He couldn't be dying. He must have just been lonely and sad and going out of his mind, living in this vast mansion all by himself. I didn't tell him that his ancestral home had filled me with unease. I wanted to listen to him talk, give him unconditional support, as had always been my job where Akshar was concerned. Against all odds, I wanted the next four days to be filled with light and warmth.

3

the woman in the room

The woman in the room used to be an artist – her work filled her with confused, angry pride. In the large extravagant canvases on which she threw herself, her thoughts, her feelings, otherwise so tightly controlled. She knew she was good. When others pointed out how striking her art was, it angered her; it seemed patronizing, like a pat on the back, a bone for a dog.

She could have been a professional, she could have made more money than her husband did. At least that's what she thought but since there was no evidence that this would have been the case, it sounded like the petulant claim of a brat. The woman had once narrowed her eyes at the nurse and said, 'I know what you are thinking. That I was just a frustrated housewife like the rest. But I wasn't. I was different. I wasn't like them.'

The nurse had smiled and shrugged. That was exactly what she had been thinking.

Then one day they went down to the room where the canvases were kept. The nurse didn't know about or understand art, but that large room contained every colour on planet earth, every stroke, every shape, under its vaulted roof. The woman's paintings pulsated with life in the stillness, told stories that were meant for those who might listen.

'I like these,' the nurse said to her patient and the woman, worn down by the years of hate and neglect, was happy with the meagre compliment. They were standing in front of a canvas on which a beautiful sky-blue Porsche was going up in flames. The car had no roof and it was raining – a torrential rain which nevertheless didn't have the power to douse the fire. And inside the roofless car a little lizard-like girl with limp, tangled hair was sitting in a white ruffled nightgown with an umbrella held primly over her head, a pretty pink one with big mauve spots. With one hand she grasped the umbrella and with the other she waved, smiling into space. The smile didn't quite reach the eyes, which were weighed down by dark circles extending halfway down her cheeks.

'What is happening in this painting?' asked the nurse, trying to make sense of a rain that couldn't stop fire and a girl who smiled inside a burning car.

'Oh, nothing,' said the woman, tossing her head back like the diva she was. 'Just life, isn't it? Just life.' The nurse smiled, reminding herself that the woman was, after all, suffering from dementia – not all there. Poor woman. All these paintings, so talented. But they were a little unhinged, these canvases, she thought. They made no sense. They were wild, bright, even beautiful, but clearly the ravings of a lunatic mind in the making. And the fires. Every second picture had flames and fire. It made the nurse uncomfortable.

'Mr Khanna, he liked my paintings, went on about how gorgeous they were and that they shouldn't be locked up like this,' said the woman with a smirk.

'Mr Ratul Khanna, who owns the cement factory?' the nurse asked. The factory had been shut down recently for its high pollution levels and other malpractices, including ill-treatment of the women workers.

'Yes, but who knows. He was just being nice perhaps – since we were having sex,' said the woman, delighting and shocking the nurse in equal measure. There had been rumours in the town about the woman and Mr Khanna, some fifteen years back. 'His penis was bigger than Avyukt's but smaller than—'

'Let's go back to the room,' said the nurse tersely, not letting her complete the sentence. A little bit of nonsense was okay, but there were limits. Mr and Mrs Khanna's son was engaged to be married. Such a scandal it would be if anyone came to know the rubbish this mad woman was spewing. The nurse hushed her and led her back to the room. She filed the information about Mr Khanna's penis away in one corner of her mind. No harm in telling her best friend about it the next time she went to town. Rita was very discreet. They could laugh about it over tea and Marie biscuits, and then get on with their day.

the woman who left

The little girl had been told her daddy was going away for a few months. She knew a euphemism when she heard one.

Vasundhara remembered that evening very clearly. She remembered how Adil dropped her off at her old house. A house she had forgotten. It had been three years, and she'd rarely met her daughter or husband in that time. She felt like a different person with her new purple-streaked hair and gym-toned body, her caterpillar unibrow threaded into two perfect manageable crescents above her eyes. They had been good, calm years, filled to the brim with Adil and love and work. She hadn't looked back. Nor thought of this house that filled her with dread. Or the daughter who had emerged from her womb in one swoop – a delivery so easy that even the doctor was surprised. A tiny lizard-like baby that was born with her beady eyes already open. She had entered the little girl's bedroom, all lilac and pretty. A white sheet was stretched across from the doorknob of the cupboard to the shelves next to the bed.

'What are you playing?' she had asked.

The girl had unknotted the sheet and carefully folded it away. Vasundhara had tried not to stare at the dot of pus that was moving on the disfigured heart-shaped lump of flesh on her daughter's collarbone. Behind the sheet that the girl had removed were all the toys of her childhood – mutilated, grotesque. Barbie dolls with plastic torsos lying at their feet, stuffed toys that bled clumps of white cotton wool from their severed necks, cars with broken windshields and torn tyres, dollhouses and kitchen utensils that had been smashed with who knows what, a rocking horse with its head rolling on the ground, the jagged wooden edges sticking out at misshapen angles.

Vasundhara had looked at the girl and the girl, pushing her tangled dirty brown hair out of her eyes, had looked straight at her mother. And then, in a gesture that never left Vasundhara till her dying day, she had lifted her right hand to her throat, her thumb tucked under her palm, and slowly drawn her index finger across it. Vasundhara knew it wasn't her own neck she was cutting off. It was her mother's.

Vasundhara had taken a step backwards. Stopped. As if stepping once again into the nightmare that she had left three years ago.

'Your father's getting married and moving to Singapore,' she had said, her voice firm and cold. 'You have to come and live with me, so get used to the idea.'

The girl's face had crumpled, just for a moment, and Vasundhara had felt a pang. For this child who was being abandoned by her father and didn't know how to love her mother. She had tentatively reached out for the little girl, but she shrank back.

'I don't want you,' the little girl had said, softly and clearly, her beady lizard eyes gleaming balefully at Vasundhara. 'I don't want to stay with you and your boyfriend.'

And I don't want you either, Vasundhara had said to herself. But that wasn't a thought she could afford. She hadn't expected the child to be easy, she never ever had had that expectation from her.

She had gone down the stairs slowly. To meet her ex-husband, who was packing pots and pans into big brown cartons in the kitchen. The girl had come down too, stood next to her dad who patted her head absentmindedly. She had put her arms around his knees. Her eyes had softened. She didn't know how to not love him. He could do no wrong. Her pasty skin had even seemed to lose its unhealthy glow as she held on to him tightly.

Vasundhara had opened the cupboard nearest to her.

'What would you like to do with these?' she had asked, met with jars that were empty, half-full or filled to the brim. It had surprised her. How neatly he had lived on his own for all those years. Alone with his daughter. The woman he was going to marry lived in Singapore. They had met online.

'Would you like to take some?' he had asked in return, pointing vaguely at containers of rice and dals. She had shrugged but taken one of the cartons and started placing the jars neatly according to size in it. They had worked in companiable silence for a while.

'Where did she go?' he had suddenly asked, looking around for his daughter.

'She was here just now ...' Vasundhara had replied, not quite paying attention.

'Yes, perhaps she went up to her room,' he had said, before his eyes wandered to the corridor and he noticed the main door was ajar. 'Vasundhara, she's outside …'

The two of them had run out but they hadn't had to go far. In the dark driveway, they could see the little girl squatting next to the car, swaying, intent on some task that she had set for herself. The shadow of the grilled main gate had fallen over the moonlit boundary walls, crisscrossing and imprisoning the crouching shadow of the girl in a way that was so cinematically beautiful that Vasundhara had found herself watching the child on the wall, a velvet moving shadow. It was there that she had seen the big kitchen knife first, its serrated edges sharper and more clear in the reflection than in reality. She had seen the knife being drawn back and then disappearing into the shadows cast by the little girl, as she had slashed the tyre in front of her with astonishing force for that tiny body.

Her dad had reached the girl. He had knelt and taken the knife out of her hand, put it down on the driveway and hugged her. The base of the tyre was a flatline, so competently had the child slashed away at it and let all the air out.

The child had broken into sobs. 'You can't go, Daddy. You can't leave …'

Vasundhara hadn't moved. She had looked at the sobbing child in the arms of her father, who seemed to be weeping too, and felt a sense of helplessness – something bordering, almost, on distaste. She remembered wishing she could just walk past the weeping father and child, out of the grilled gate, and never come back. Away from that façade of a family that had been her life three years back and was threatening to overwhelm her once again.

the woman who was unafraid of fire

My room was on the third floor. Akshar lived on the second. There was a long corridor like in a hotel, doors leading off it. I unpacked my suitcase and put everything in the large oak cupboard. It was a beautiful, spacious room with an ornate four-poster bed and rugs on the wooden floor. The view from the window was glorious and lonely, the distant mountain ranges partially shrouded with mist. I can never settle down in a new place if I don't unpack properly, even on short visits. But despite how aesthetically pleasing my room was I didn't feel like spending time there. I took a quick bath and headed down to find Akshar.

Akshar had said he would be in his study on the ground floor where he usually spent his afternoons. I made my way down the dank corridors and many flights of stairs. If Akshar had stayed alone in a pretty little cottage in the hills it would have been easier somehow. Until I arrived here, I hadn't imagined what it would mean to find a single person living all alone in a huge mansion where even the main gate seemed to be a kilometre away from the house, effectively cutting off communication with the rest of the town.

The quiet and efficient Ravinder silently materialized on the first-floor landing and directed me towards Akshar's study. I was pleasantly surprised to find a messy, cheerful, lived-in room where the rays of the setting sun lit up the pinewood bookshelves, the couch with a colourful paisley print along one wall decorated with a photograph of young Akshar and his father in front of a bonfire, the many small tables which were overflowing with curios and books and the enormous desk behind which Akshar was sitting. But in the unexpected brightness of the study Akshar seemed somewhat depleted and insubstantial. I hadn't noticed when we were upstairs how straggly and oversized his knitted black sweater was. The Akshar I knew was much into appearances, but it didn't seem like he cared very much anymore.

'Akshar, did you eat?' Ravinder had served us parathas upstairs before I went to take a bath. I'd gobbled down two but Akshar had said he'd had a heavy breakfast.

Akshar smiled, his grey-green eyes crinkling up at the sides, but I didn't feel reassured. The crow's feet seemed lopsided, the lines pulled downwards and not in the pretty fan design I remembered. Everything about Akshar was a little off now, physically and otherwise.

'I don't eat much anymore, Shalini,' he said. 'Are you hungry though?'

'Not yet, I'll tell you when I am,' I replied. 'What are you reading?'

'Nothing new.' He held up a tattered copy of *Discipline and Punish*.

'How many times must you read that?' The question was one of affectionate familiarity but my tone was querulous, causing Akshar to raise his eyebrows.

'As many times as I want to?' he quipped, mirthless. 'Did you meet Sahil? He stays on the ground floor.'

'Sahil, your brother? I thought he was outside the country.' I remembered Sahil as a supercilious, unpleasant kid. But I supposed it was nice that Akshar wasn't all alone as I had thought.

'He had an accident. Came here three months ago, and hasn't gone back since,' Akshar said.

'What accident?'

'A fire in Birmingham where he was at the time. One of the first of these fires – too few at the time for people to get alarmed.'

'Oh,' I said and ran out of words. It was all too much to process.

'When he told me a fire sprang up in the middle of the road, I asked him if he was doing drugs,' Akshar laughed, though I couldn't see the humour. 'He had to get skin grafts on his legs and came home when he was well enough to leave the hospital.'

'Why didn't you tell me this?'

'I am telling you this,' he shrugged. So easily we had regressed to familiar childhood patterns of punctuating every conversation with impatience and bickering. I didn't really want to know more about the fire in Birmingham.

'It must be nice to have Sahil around. This mansion is so big and ...' I didn't complete the sentence. Akshar loved his home and my thoughts weren't complimentary.

'*This mansion is so big*,' Akshar mimicked. 'And so I should fill the empty rooms with anyone and everyone.'

I felt winded by his sarcasm. I guess I was out of practice. 'I don't know how you are with your brother now. I never got your relationship with him in any case.'

'There are many things about me you have never understood, Shalini,' he said. Which was unfair. I'd spent a lifetime trying to understand him.

'At least I have tried,' I replied. 'I don't think you've ever cared to even *try* to get me, Akshar.'

'I get you. It's easy to get you. You are more transparent than you think.'

'Are you mocking me?'

'No, I love that about you – the lack of artifice.' I wanted to laugh out loud. No one saw me as a straightforward, easygoing person. But it was also true that with Akshar I had always been compliant, needy – he could reach out and pluck my soul in a minute.

'It looks like the sun will set soon. Can we sit outside for a bit?' I asked, not just to change the subject. Few things in nature are as beautiful as the dipping sun drawing a dark blanket over jagged mountain tops. It was exactly as lovely outside as I had expected. The hilltops shrouded in mist, the sky a perfect deep blue. In the distance, the sound of bells tinkling and conches being blown.

'The staff quarters,' said Akshar, pointing at a block of rectangular rooms further down the hill from us. On the roof stood a group of women in vibrant patterned maxis, looking skyward, ululating in harmony with the bells and conches.

'They are offering prayers to the rain gods, to stop the fires worldwide,' Akshar explained. 'It's a local custom that the women in these parts practise as the sun sets, any time there's a natural disaster that we hear of, anywhere in the world.'

'Oh, that's beautiful.' I was moved by the simplicity of it. A quiet ritual of collective action to restore balance in the natural world that didn't make it to the headlines.

'It is,' said Akshar. 'Those are Ravinder and Jai Singh's wives and their friends and daughters. But where is Ravinder? He should be here.'

The valley was echoing with the faint sounds of bells and women's voices, though we could only see those on the rooftop near us. Akshar's mansion was too isolated, the grounds too large. Even his next-door neighbour would have been a mile or so away. Akshar muttered something about Ravinder and teatime and marched off towards the staff quarters.

He was back in a few minutes. I could see Ravinder hurrying behind him. It was a steep climb from the staff quarters to where I was. I would have been panting and straining but Akshar, despite his sallow complexion and general air of ill health, was striding up effortlessly. He belonged to the mountains, to the inclines and sharp corners that marked the hillsides.

'Fucking idiot. Smoking up happily, no work ethic.' Akshar's tone was harsh. His quick judgements, impatience – I was used to them but I was older too now; I couldn't be as forgiving or adoring as I was before. I wasn't particularly impressed by Akshar parading around as the monarch of all he surveyed.

'He surely would have showed up. What's the hurry?' I stopped as I saw a shadow on my left and turned to find Ravinder standing behind me. A resentful gaze met the smile I gave him.

'Ravinder, serve dinner in my study please. At 7 p.m.,' Akshar said and turned to me. 'It's the women in this town, Shalini, who do all the work. They speak up against injustices. You know, the usual. Industrial, patriarchal.' Forces that you stand for, I almost said but didn't. I wanted us to be peaceful, not sparring from the get-go. He didn't say anything more either. The sun had almost disappeared between the distant hills and we sat quietly watching the sky, striped in impossible reds, pinks and greys that leaked into each other. The inkiness of night wiped and subsumed the brightness of day as it would again, relentlessly, twenty-four hours later. There was comfort in that thought.

'Let's go in,' Akshar said, getting up. 'Tell me about this guy you are dating.'

'When did I tell you …' I hadn't mentioned Mukul at all.

'You didn't but don't forget how well I know you,' Akshar replied. I suspected it was just a shot in the dark but still.

'Well, he has a lovely voice, a deep baritone – you know me and how important that is. And he's just very nice. He's caring. Charming, assured.' So many adjectives, each of them begging stories and elaborations.

'Say more.'

'You know, like, he really listens when I talk? Which is so rare.'

'I don't?' asked Akshar, inserting himself with ease into the conversation. As he always did.

'Let's talk about you then,' I said. Akshar laughed, a little sheepish. 'You don't really want to know about Mukul, do you?'

'How long have you been together?' he asked without replying but I didn't want to answer his question either. Akshar only understood lifetimes of togetherness. He would laugh if I said a few months.

'Never mind, Akshar, really,' I said. 'But now *you* tell me – Aahana? Where is she?'

'Aahana,' Akshar repeated. 'You'll meet her tomorrow. She always comes over on Mondays.'

I hadn't expected that. Just like that, I was going to meet her. Akshar had slipped it in as if it was nothing. I had always thought of her as a princess locked away in a tower, who Akshar kept away from the world. Whenever I had asked if I would ever get to meet her in the past he had shrugged. I wanted to ask so many questions now. What did it mean that she visited him every week?

'I bumped into a doctor on the staircase in the morning. Was he …'

'Yes, he was,' Akshar said.

'Yes, he was what?' I pressed. It was exasperating, the way Akshar would economize with words sometimes, just to tease or so it seemed to me.

'Aahana's husband,' he said. 'The doctor, the doctor. Which brings us to why I asked you to come.'

I still had so many questions about Aahana but Akshar was the one steering the conversation, moving from one topic to another, and now it seemed we would talk about his health. Which was indeed why I had come in the first place – because he was dying. I had firmly kept the thought at the back of my mind since the morning. Standing in front of him, reaching out and touching his arm or hugging him, it seemed inconceivable – a bag of bones he was, yes, but no, he couldn't be dying.

Akshar's customary glibness faltered as he started talking about his health. His voice kept changing from tremulous indecision to energetic precision in a way that I remembered very well. He had always been prone to speak in this manner when he got into one of his moods. He spoke in sentences that were convoluted. I had to strain to follow but I got the gist of it, if not the finer details.

Akshar had a rare genetic disorder – a strain of thalassemia that was often known to be fatal. It was the reason why he never left the hills for prolonged periods. He had had the disease for five years now but doctors – both in India and abroad – were beginning to give up. The weekly blood transfusions that had been sustaining him for over a year now were no longer yielding results.

I listened, I tried to understand the pauses, I strained to hear the whispers as he grew tired of speaking and seemed too exhausted to continue. Then again, suddenly, he would raise his voice, octave by octave, till he was practically shouting at me. Strange medical jargon, fear of dying, philosophical railings against his inability to make anything of a life that he had had high hopes for in the days when teachers and professors had declared him a prodigy.

I had heard him speak in this way before. But this was an exaggerated, operatic version of his old style of delivery. 'It's my mother's fault and all the women before her,' he said all of a sudden and when I asked what that meant, he murmured something about the fires, the women and all he had inherited. It was stupefying. I slumped in my chair; all the questions I had drained out of my system, leaving me blank.

I felt cold and found I was shivering a little, though the temperature hadn't dropped. I was glad when Ravinder knocked at the door and came in with a skinny, pimply boy wheeling a trolley laden with platters of food, plates and cutlery. For the next forty-five minutes, we focused on eating the delicious shepherd's pie, soft bread rolls baked to perfection and a Boston cream pie with a perfect layer of cream, semi-solid and unsweetened, and a chocolate ganache topping. Akshar told me about his fancy chef, who had been trained at a patisserie in Delhi but returned to the hills because his family lived there.

Everyone returned to these hills it seemed. Sahil didn't join us and I didn't particularly care to see him either.

After dinner Akshar seemed less agitated. The way he had spoken had unsettled me; the unease of the morning when I had stood in front of the mansion had returned. But I willed myself to feel calm again. We listened to music, rehashed old memories and didn't talk about all that was urgent and immediate. We had a few more days together and there was time yet. For all the difficult thoughts to be aired, for revisiting the complications of the past and imagining a future that might not have Akshar in it.

The next morning I found my way to the dining room, which was at one end of the ground floor. I had woken up to a text from Akshar saying he was having breakfast and that I was to meet him there. It was a long, rectangular room with French windows along one wall, opening onto a strip of lawn. A solitary marble table with twenty chairs, with a huge crystal chandelier hanging over it, dominated the room. It was a grand and dreary space, and to see Akshar sitting alone at the head of the table didn't take away from the sad, anachronistic feel of a century past – of some parodic version of Mrs Havisham that Dickens might have approved of. But looking away from the gloom of peeling plaster and heavy velvet drapes and more closely at Akshar, sitting on a large, throne-like mahogany chair, I changed my mind. His appearance yesterday might have been more in line with Mrs Havisham in her decaying wedding gown but today he looked surprisingly fresh and dapper. He had washed his hair and was wearing a stylish brown leather jacket.

'Morning, Shalini. Come, sit. What will you have? Mondays are special for me. The rest of the week goes by somehow but today is my Aahana day,' he said, putting a forkful of grapefruit into his mouth.

I felt a sharp stab of childhood jealousy. I had forgotten the feeling, but it was back in an instant – a flare of envy that was physical in its intensity and made me feel hot and dizzy for a few long seconds. Not that I was competing anymore – he was welcome to his Aahana day – but I had arrived yesterday from far away, and he was seeing me after five long years. Still, it hadn't been a special day for him. He had been lounging in tattered clothes, unbothered about his appearance when I arrived. Yet I'd found him beautiful. So stupid. I remembered once more how he had told me there was nothing romantic between Aahana and him anymore – wasn't that some ten years back? And she had married the cold-eyed doctor some time last year, many years after Akshar and Aahana broke up. But here he was again. Still infatuated, living only for her visits, dying in the days in between. Like an old-fashioned lover from a nineteenth-century Gothic romance. It didn't add up, none of it made sense.

'When will she come?' I asked, sitting down on the chair to Akshar's left. Ravinder had materialized out of nowhere to take my breakfast order. I asked for eggs benedict on Akshar's urging – apparently the chef made it really well.

'In an hour – at 11 a.m. That's when she always comes.'

'Without the doctor husband I presume?' I asked, and Akshar, missing the fact that I was being sarcastic in his heightened state of anticipation, launched eagerly into an explanation. 'He goes to a neighbouring town every Monday – it's two hours away. Returns late at night. Sometimes the next morning if he has too many patients there.' How very convenient and wonderful and baffling. Baffling for me, at least. Why had Akshar, instead of marrying his childhood sweetheart, claimed the romance was dead while proceeded with this Monday arrangement that obviously meant the world to him?

I didn't have the answers but when, at exactly 11 a.m., Aahana swept into the room, I could see what it was that would draw anyone to her. It wasn't just how beautiful she was – tall, elegant and regal – but her heart-shaped face and grey-green eyes exuded this warmth and perfection that was irresistible.

Akshar introduced us and Aahana put one beautifully manicured hand with long red nails on my arm and said warmly, 'Shalini, we meet at last. I've heard so much about you for the last ... well, forever really. Ever since Akshar went to boarding school.' Her voice was hushed, the words came gliding out with quick little stresses and pauses, in one breath.

It pleased me when she said that. In spite of everything, I had never felt like I was consequential to Akshar's life. He drew me towards him when needed and I was always there for him because I didn't know how not to be.

Akshar put an arm around Aahana's shoulders and asked softly, 'Are you okay?' It was then that I noticed what I should have right when she entered the room. Her stomach was huge. She was pregnant and to my inexperienced eyes, it seemed that the baby might pop out any minute. Akshar put one hand on her stomach, his eyes soft with love. Aahana smiled and patted his cheek and between them everything was as I had always imagined it to be – perfect and sublime, the most connected couple ever.

Except. Wasn't she married to someone else? And this baby would be her husband's no matter how lovingly Akshar might caress her tummy! It was all just so bizarre.

'Let's get some fresh air?' Aahana was looking at me. I nodded. We stepped onto the strip of lawn outside the dining room. I hadn't seen a gardener yet, but there had to be a competent one – the house was surrounded by flowerbeds that were a riot of colours. I couldn't identify most of them but resolved to take photographs for my dad. He regularly spent hours planting and weeding his pocket-sized lawn and devoted all his spare time to gardening; his front porch and backyard were full of potted plants and creepers too.

Aahana and Akshar sat on the two-seater swing while I perched on one of the cushioned benches. The view was lovely – emerald mountains, turquoise skies and terraced hillslopes dotted with cottages.

Aahana and Akshar were a cliché that worked so well. The way Aahana spoke, what she said, her vivacity – she was a feminine version of Akshar. She was all female in the way that Akshar was all male. She had Akshar's curiosity but tempered with warmth; his knowledge of literature and politics but softened with humility; his sense of humour but not as scathing; his way of looking at the world but with less certainty.

It was unsurprising. Of course a person as driven by self-love as Akshar would feel true love only towards his mirror image, and that too the stereotypically feminine version of it. Sitting on that swing they looked like twins – the aquiline nose, grey-green eyes, thin and shapely red lips, the same gangly frame (apart from her humongous stomach). Or perhaps to my unpracticed eye all mountain people looked the same! Ravinder and Jai Singh had similar features, too. I felt disgust at the way Akshar and Aahana sat, hands casually intertwined, so wrapped up in themselves and each other. It seemed delusional and devoid of reality.

Yesterday had been disorienting – the revelations about Akshar's health, the unnatural, decaying splendour of this mansion. But I'd had a good night's rest and woken up feeling rested, loving the freshness of the mountain air. Now even the idea of two more days was stifling. I had chatted with Mukul before falling asleep last night and ended the call with a perfunctory 'I miss you' I hadn't quite meant. Yet all of a sudden, I missed him with an intensity I hadn't felt before. I wanted to be back where I belonged – in Delhi, in my little messy, pretty apartment, with my graphic novels and plants and paintings. A life that I'd painstakingly built for myself.

'Are you okay, Shalini?' Aahana asked. And then, turning to Akshar, 'Let's go for a drive? You know, show Shalini the town. What say?'

'I don't know,' said Akshar. 'You're the one who's been saying we should be careful because of the fires …'

'Yes, but I am tired of living like that. I just drove here, and there's been no fire on the mountain roads yet. We have to get out, we can't be scared like this,' Aahana said, her voice rising a little.

'I am not scared at all. Meanwhile, you freaked when you heard about the fire in town, and that was so far from here.' Akshar laughed, putting his hand on her thigh and rubbing it up and down. When Aahana pouted, he relented and said, 'Okay, let's go.'

'It's so pretty here,' I interjected. 'I don't mind staying in. Why don't you guys go – I feel carsick so easily in the hills. I'll just get my laptop and finish some work.'

'Oh no, of course not,' said Aahana. 'I want to show you the town. Once we get out of the car and walk around in the mall, you won't feel sick.'

Akshar gave me a sideways glance that was reproving. We must do what Aahana wanted, I supposed.

I felt childish and petty for being the party pooper when she with her unnaturally large tummy was happy to brave the fires and go gallivanting. 'Alright then, let's go!' I said, a little too loudly and cheerfully. Aahana clapped her hands and stood up, saying, 'That's more like it! Yay! Get up, Aksh.'

Akshar drove with Aahana in the passenger seat while I lounged at the back. It took us a while to get out of Akshar's property – down the winding road to that faraway main gate. The town was picturesque as promised. The winding mall road had quaint little shops on one side and a lovely view of distant peaks on the other.

'Oh, Akshar,' I said, leaning out of the window and doing my best to stay in the moment. 'There's that photo studio – is it still run by that eccentric man, I forget his name?'

They both laughed. 'Yes, Dr D as we call him. Dubey-ji to the rest,' said Akshar. 'Let me park here.'

As we got out of the car, I saw Akshar and Aahana exchange a look I couldn't quite decipher. Striding up to us was a skinny young fellow, dark with large lustrous curls that fell on his forehead and a smile that was dimpled and pretty.

'Hi Sahil,' Aahana said, not looking too pleased. 'We could have come together – we didn't know you were going to be here too.'

'Oh, is this Shalini?' Sahil laughed, ignoring her niceties. The dimples reappeared, but they didn't look pretty anymore. 'The last time I met you was on the day that dog died.'

I felt a wave rising in front of my eyes, like the grey static on a TV screen in the olden days. For a moment I couldn't breathe. *That little boy running around our school premises. The day that Jugaad died in a fire that sprung up in the gatekeeper's cottage. Jugaad, caught in that fire. We found his body. His poor little body. I screamed and screamed, a scream that seemed to live inside me for days. And this little boy, Sahil. Running around the cottage in circles as if nothing had happened. Laughing. Just like he was laughing now.*

'Hello Sahil. I would never have recognized you,' I said, trying to bring my thoughts back to the present.

'Considering I was five when we met, that's obvious, isn't it?' he replied. I felt a wave of intense dislike. He would be about twenty-two now – lanky and tall like his brother but there the similarity ended. They didn't look like siblings. I remembered Akshar telling me about an ugly family fight during which his dad had said Sahil was not his son and his mother had just laughed and not bothered to deny it.

'My brother, so charming,' said Akshar, and Aahana laughed. I felt marginally better.

'Should we go to Romania?' asked Aahana. Turning to me, she added, 'It's a café – relax, Shalini. Good coffee and carrot cake.'

'See y'all,' said Sahil, walking off in the other direction. Thankfully. It was clear that Aahana didn't care for Sahil either.

Romania had wood-panelled walls with cute messages and artwork, colourful cushions and carpets. The café was packed – all the tables were occupied and there was much jostling at the cash counter. The weekend before I left Delhi a group of us from office had gone to a pub in a nearby mall. The parking lot was deserted, with only a handful of restaurants open. The pub which usually bustled insanely on Friday evenings was practically empty too. It was eerie. We didn't stay long. It felt irresponsible to be partying in the midst of a global catastrophe that needed to be fixed. Clearly the people in this hill station felt no such compunctions.

Akshar and I ordered lattes and Aahana a green tea, with slices of carrot cake and apple pie. There was seating outside as well. We went down a spiral staircase to a back lawn, where there was a gazebo.

'Akshar, Aahana,' said a young woman with a toddler, coming up to our table. 'So good to see you guys. When's the baby due?'

My sense of discomfort had stopped me from acknowledging Aahana's pregnancy – I had studiously avoided asking her any question about the obvious.

'Very soon,' said Aahana. 'About a month to go.'

'Take care though. The mall road is always so crowded,' said the young woman. 'And with everything that's going on in the world ...'

'No fires here so far though, we're all good,' Akshar replied cheerfully.

'I just heard of one, not on the mall road but higher up, near the church ... one girl got severe burns, and this boy who managed to pull her out is also in hospital now.' The woman seemed to hesitate and then added, 'Dr Qureshi will know, of course.'

'He mentioned,' said Aahana carelessly, as if it didn't matter. Akshar looked at her sharply and seemed about to say something then changed his mind.

'Are you excited about the baby?' I asked after the woman and her child left. A polite question to show that I had noticed she was pregnant.

'Under the circumstances … I'm not so sure, Shalini,' said Aahana. I didn't want to ask what that meant. Akshar ignored our exchange and addressed Aahana, 'Why did you tell me there had been no cases here, Aahana? That's just irresponsible. We shouldn't be out and about then.'

'Don't be silly, Akshar,' Aahana said impatiently. 'Anyway, we are sitting in a café now.'

'Better to be cautious, wouldn't you say?' Akshar said. 'In your condition especially.'

'And yours?' Aahana's eyes were suddenly glittering with tears, and she leaned towards him. 'I don't give a fuck about silly fires or anything else when you won't even show me your medical records anymore. Aksh, you know I can't live without you. I want to die.'

'Don't. Ever. Say. That.' Akshar spoke through gritted teeth and there was such desperation on his face that

I had to look away. I felt like I was spying on them through a keyhole – they were that oblivious of my presence. Aahana pushed her chair back and got up, so hard that it toppled over and the people at the next table gave her startled looks. She marched off and was halfway up the spiral staircase by the time I picked up the chair and looked at Akshar, who hadn't even got up. He was staring vacantly into space, seemingly unaware of Aahana's dramatic exit.

We found Aahana leaning against the car. Akshar was in front of me when I caught my foot in something. I stumbled a little and looked down, feeling a strange sort of weariness. My eyes felt hot. I could feel these waves of heat around me. The road was heating up too, burning really. My feet felt scalded, I took a few steps backward involuntarily and found it wasn't that hot anymore but in front of me there were flames, small flames, licking at the ground. Red, orange, yellow flames. They started flaring up and suddenly, there was this big fire, like a wall in front of me.

I felt a sense of despair that seemed to well up from somewhere deep within me. I saw Jugaad's little body, broken by fire; a fire that had to do its job, had to annihilate. It was the only way.

I closed my eyes. I could sense evil, the horrifying ways of a world gone rogue, that didn't know peace, that maimed animals, that snatched away livelihoods, that destroyed all that was organic, splendid and natural. What could be done? I knew we had no choice but to succumb, to accept the fire. I felt a cosmic sorrow like nothing I had experienced before – or had I not? It had always been there inside me, this ball of fire and anguish, crushing my bones, making me breathless.

I opened my eyes. The despair lifted or became bearable at least. The wall of fire had become larger; there was no sky above, simply vertical rivers of shimmering fire. I couldn't look away. I stared at the heat, the flames, and in that moment all sorts of images swam in front of my eyes – memories from my childhood, like snapshots, visions through a kaleidoscope, moving quickly, spinning, like the fire was burning only for me, it comprised my life, my thoughts. It was strange, it was gorgeous, and I took a few tentative steps forward, towards the fire.

I don't know what happened in the next few moments but all at once, I was being pulled backwards. I snapped out of my trance-like state and felt relief, gratitude. I was safe. Akshar had put his arms around my waist and dragged me away from the fire.

There was chaos all around. A lot of people were running away, some were rooted to the ground the way I had been and there was one man who took determined steps and landed right in the middle of the fire. And then he screamed and screamed as the flames licked at him greedily, consuming him.

Aahana was sitting inside the car with her head in her hands. She didn't ask me what had happened. My mind was an incoherent mess, and I couldn't have verbalized it in any case. Akshar pushed me into the backseat and before I knew it, he drove off. He was honking madly, trying to weave past pedestrians, bikes, cars and tempo travelers, all helter-skelter with panic. I saw Sahil too, at the edge of the street, staring away from the fire, at the hills on the other side of the valley. I was sure Akshar saw him but he didn't stop – he drove as fast as was possible, away from the mall road.

None of us said a word on our way back. I made my excuses on reaching the house, mumbled something and went off to my room. I lay down on the large four-poster bed and tried to gather my feelings. I had no idea what had happened. Perhaps Akshar had saved me but I felt more distant from him than ever before. I was exhausted, the fire had depleted me.

I went into the bathroom for a hot shower. I felt unclean. I looked at my face in the ornate antique mirror as I took my clothes off and dumped them in the wicker basket for washing. My hair hung limp and dry, my skin looked drab and spotty with the dark circles under my eyes more pronounced than ever. I stepped into the shower cubicle. The bathroom was filled with steam as I stood under a jet of scalding water, not tempering it with cold water, letting the blistering wetness wash the day right off my skin. There was a clump of hair blocking the drain. I had been losing a lot of hair lately. I thought of Aahana's lustrous and thick chestnut brown hair, piled into a careless-careful bun on top of her head.

I thought of Akshar – his life, our life, the times we had spent together. I knew most of the images I'd seen in the fire were of Akshar – young Akshar in our school blazer, Akshar throwing a stick for Jugaad to fetch … Akshar calling out to me from the flames, asking me to join him. I felt self-loathing. Here he was, going about with Aahana as if I hardly existed. Magnanimously allowing me to be a spectator to the grand spectacle that was his life. I needed to stay at a remove, follow the twists and turns in the Akshar–Aahana dynamic with morbid interest at best. I couldn't afford to feel anything more than that. Not anymore. Never again.

When I looked back, I felt sorry for myself and the way I had acted through all my boarding school years – and beyond, too, perhaps. So brave and helpless, so selflessly in love. If I had a therapist today, perhaps she would say my inability to fall in love was tied up with that childhood rejection, to always coming second with Akshar.

I wondered about Dr Qureshi, whether he was similarly infatuated with Aahana – a neat parallel to me with Akshar. But we never held a chance, Qureshi or me. For a moment I felt empathetically drawn towards the moist-eyed doctor. But then he had got to marry his love. If that mattered. Though why did Aahana marry him when she was so clearly in love with Akshar?

Anyway, I had had enough. I was okay to live without the answers to all the unresolved strands of the Aahana–Akshar love story. I could just go home now. A part of me was still glad I had come. It had given me the closure I'd never got, which I'd always desperately craved. It was unreal and tragic, this strange love story, this beautiful but eerie mansion, the loneliness and solitude of the lofty mountain peaks. I felt the burning hot water enter my pores, my body filling with water and fire, cold heat inside me, replacing all my organs, making me bloated, shapeless, ugly, fearful. I quickly turned the knob to stop the water. I touched my body, my arms, my shoulders. All good, all there. I forced myself to calm down. Everything was fine. I would be home soon. And I would build my life again. Like I always had.

4

the woman in the room

Some days the woman forgot to be bitter. She thought of Avyukt Gupta as she had first known him. The laughter especially; it surprised her to remember how much they had laughed together. The early mock fights, the petty jealousies that had seemed to spell love. The tears, the rages that ended in kisses. Much before it all turned inward and festered and there was no chance in hell of a resolution.

The woman remembered the first time she met Meher. They had been married for three years. Avyukt had told her that his ex-girlfriend, Meher, would be at the party they were going to. The woman had dutifully pretended to mind, more to tease her husband than anything. Of course, it didn't matter. She knew he only had eyes for her.

She remembered that day clearly. Meher, in her beautiful *firozi* pink *phiran*, with intricate white threadwork, a pink cocktail with one of those tiny paper umbrellas in one hand, in the long, open veranda of the club, the sky blue and powdery behind her.

'I've been dying to meet you, Disha,' said Meher when they were introduced, all warm and friendly, and Disha couldn't help but like her. They had met her husband Aman for the first time that afternoon too, a Merchant Navy officer. Avyukt and Aman had made plans to play golf together. Meher and Disha had said they would tag along and go swimming. The four of them had become fast friends after that lunch party. They had hung out on weekends at each other's houses, drank copious quantities of wine, played Scrabble and Taboo.

Disha didn't quite know when Avyukt and Meher had started having an affair – or re-started, as the case may be. Though there was something innocent and sweet about childhood sweethearts, what happened in the years that followed was anything but. In retrospect, what had angered her most was that she had been clueless, not even one bit suspicious. Reading the books Meher recommended, watching movies together, exchanging gossip. But Disha had also not been fully present in her own life in those days. She had started painting again, after a hiatus of seven or eight years, and when she painted her mind shifted; it became a rollercoaster of seesawing colours, of a deep solitude that needed no one, of soft and hard brushes, of endless tubes of paint that she couldn't get enough of. If her mother-in-law asked her to put lilies in a crystal flower vase she didn't hear or care, if Avyukt wanted her to choose which shirt he should wear for the neighbour's party it maddened her – the inanity of the question, the neediness he sometimes showed. If Avyukt forced her to go out she would often be sullen and withdrawn, her heart a big red splash left behind on the half-finished canvas at home. But then Meher, sunny and charming, would draw her out to the balcony for a smoke, she would tell her how deathly dull the party had been till Avyukt and she had arrived. Disha had enjoyed being with Meher in a way that she never had with any friend before.

The early years, in retrospect, had been good. The woman in the room, looking out at a barred world from her window, wondered if she should feel grateful that those years had at least given her some degree of happiness. But after a while she couldn't hold on to any of it anymore, the good or the bad. The past faded, her mind coiled up into a spiral of nothingness and she ceased to give a fuck.

the woman who left

The little girl willed herself to become a marble statue, a brick wall, a lamppost, when Adil or Vasundhara were in the room. Adil did his best. He tried to win her over with jokes, with stories of his own boyhood days, he cooked pasta for her and made smiley faces with spaghetti.

'Give her time,' Vasundhara said. It had been six months. She had told herself Adil and she had enough love between them to ride it out. But it was hard, the stony presence of a spindly little girl with unnatural dark circles who didn't give an inch. Adil didn't tell Vasundhara that her daughter was beginning to wear him out and she in turn never told him the child had never belonged to her, not from the day she was born. Adil assumed it had not been this way before Vasundhara left, the relationship between mother and daughter – the resentment, the silences, the refusal to respond. The girl must have felt abandoned when her mother left and couldn't forgive her yet. Or him for taking her mother away from her. That made sense to him, he could understand it. But he didn't know how long he could live with it. Her silent, polite presence at the dining table, her quiet steps in the corridors, the blank, cold eyes that swallowed his every overture and reduced it to nothing. It had been exactly this way from the day she had moved in with them.

Three months in, they went to visit Adil's mother in the Andamans. When they had first planned the trip, Adil had assumed the little girl would thaw by the time they arrived in Port Blair; that the holiday would help her adjust to her new family, that the coastal air and ocean would work wonders on her pasty skin. Adil's mother was so fond of children too and was dying to meet Vasundhara's daughter.

'We are going to go in a glass-bottom boat, and you will be amazed by all the fish and sea life under the surface of the ocean,' Adil said to the girl as she sat in the seat between Vasundhara and him on the flight. The girl turned the page of her picture book as if he hadn't spoken.

'That sounds so exciting,' said Vasundhara brightly from the other side of the girl. Adil and she smiled at each other over the girl's head. 'I think she will love the sea and the sand and building sandcastles.'

'Only with my father,' the little girl said clearly and loudly, taking a sideways glance at her mother. 'I don't want to go anywhere without him.'

The holiday was a disaster. Vasundhara, Adil and his mother did their best but after a couple of days, their laughter was strained, their conversations brittle under the watchful beady eyes of the lizard-like girl. She was never rude. She complied and went along with every plan like a particularly well-trained robot. She was always there, a quiet presence, but she reached out for no one and nothing. And then one night she sleepwalked into her mother's bedroom and stood at the foot of the bed while Vasundhara and Adil, unaware and oblivious, moaned in the throes of orgasm that – for the moment at least – had driven every other thought out of their minds.

As Adil turned to lie on his back, he saw the quiet little figure standing there. His mind blanked out and he couldn't speak, even as he fumbled with the sheet in a silly valiant attempt to protect himself from those glassy eyes that seemed to be boring into him.

By the time Vasundhara managed to drag on some clothes, pick up the little figure and take her back to her room, the girl was awake. Vasundhara tucked her into her bed, murmuring as lovingly as she knew how all the while. Her fist was clenched. Vasundhara gently prised open her fingers and removed the matchbox she had been clutching. The girl turned her back on her mother and went back to sleep.

'Didn't we lock the door? I forgot she sleepwalks,' Vasundhara asked when she was back in bed with Adil, holding him tight, trying to push what had just happened out of her mind.

'I thought we did,' Adil said. He stroked her hair absentmindedly but whenever Vasundhara looked back on her years with Adil, she thought of that night in Port Blair as the moment she started to lose him. The night of the fire was still a year away but their relationship was no longer the light and glorious thing it once had been. It was all beginning to fade, and it was only a matter of time before things would fall apart for good.

the woman who was unafraid of fire

I wasn't thinking about the fire. I wasn't letting my mind go there. I lay on my stomach on the bed with my laptop in front of me, mechanically ploughing through a pile of pending deadlines. My neck muscles started aching and I rolled onto my back, abandoning all pretence of work. I replied to a couple of messages that Mukul had sent earlier in the day. He replied immediately. My thoughts were scattered, my words messy and he said rather curtly that I sounded evasive. It wasn't the fire – I hadn't told him about it anyway. Too much had happened in the last twenty-four hours. It felt all too obscure and weird; I didn't have the words to convey my unease and discomfort.

My phone beeped again. This time it was a message from Akshar. Come down, it said. What a surprise: Akshar summoning me peremptorily as always but at least from the next room this time, not across hundreds of miles like last week! And down I would go, as meekly as I'd come running uphill yesterday. Akshar's favourite doormat.

I made my way down the dark corridor and stairs hoping Aahana had left, knowing she would be there.

They were sitting on the strip of lawn where we had been that morning. Aahana looked drawn and tired but younger and more vulnerable. Her long hair was no longer in a bun. She had removed her make-up and had a beautiful embroidered shawl around her frail shoulders. She looked less manicured, more open and untamed like the hills she belonged to.

'Tea, Shalini?' she asked, leaning forward and removing the tea-cosy from the pot. 'It's still hot.'

'Thanks!' I said, pouring myself a cup, looking at the sky behind her and the way the sun was slowly plunging down between the hills. It would be dark in five minutes at the most.

'What were you doing?' asked Akshar.

'Some office work – had to send off these creatives for a client.'

'Do you enjoy your work?'

'Yes, I think I do. I like the freedom I have to create – with certain restrictions, but that's the challenge.' I was surprised that Akshar was, at the end of a confusing day, making trite conversation. The part of me that craved Akshar against my better judgement was happy he was engaging with me and my life outside of himself even when Aahana was there.

She was checking her messages and frowning. 'Reyhan is on his way home. He knows there was a fire and says he might be needed at the hospital here. He'll freak if he realizes we were there.'

'We shouldn't have gone out today, Aahana, really,' he chided.

'I know what happened was weird, but we are all good now, right?' I felt guilty suddenly, as if it was my fault the fire had singled me out. I was glad neither of them had asked what I'd gone through in those few moments before Akshar had pulled me back. Or perhaps it didn't strike them at all – everything had happened quickly enough; how would they guess that the fire had reached out to me in ways I didn't want to think about?

'It's early days yet. Things are going to get bad soon. Like in the US and UK,' Akshar said, grimly.

'We are fine, it's okay,' Aahana muttered, rolling her eyes. 'Anyway, I should go home now. I'll probably be under house arrest from tomorrow.'

'When's the baby due?' I asked.

'In about a month,' she replied.

'Are you excited?' And then I remembered I'd already had this conversation with her. Not like I cared.

'More anxious than excited.'

I smiled and nodded unsurely. Aahana got up. I

supposed I would never meet her again, not on this trip or ever, for that matter.

'It was lovely meeting you, even if too briefly for my liking,' Aahana said. There were tears in her eyes. I was taken aback. She saw my surprise and brushed them away. 'I think it's the pregnancy hormones. I wasn't always so bad, was I, Aksh?'

'You were always exactly this bad, Aahana,' Akshar said tenderly, as if her tears won her some award for sensitivity and loveliness or something.

'I feel like we've always known each other, Aahana.' I tried to match her heightened emotions at our parting. 'Take care of yourself and good luck.'

I couldn't get myself to say I hoped we'd meet again. There are limits to hypocrisy.

'Let's move to the living room, Shalini,' said Akshar. 'I'll see Aahana off to her car and come.'

I nodded and made my way into the house. The living room was large and draughty despite the massive fireplace. The walls were a drab pistachio green, decorated with faded oil paintings of grim men and women – Akshar's forefathers presumably. I wished Akshar had suggested sitting in his bright and cosy study instead.

I wandered over to the bookcase in the corner and took out a dusty volume of Maupassant's collected works. My grandfather's favourite author. This mansion, reeking of nostalgia and history and gloom, was the right place to revisit one's dead grandparents, through their literary choices or otherwise.

I was reading 'The Necklace' and was more than halfway through the story – which I remembered well enough – when Akshar came into the room. It was a long goodbye he had bid his beloved. He looked haggard once again; his hair was in an untidy ponytail. It was as if Aahana was the keeper of his vitality and freshness and took them away with her when she left.

'How come you don't have a dog, Akshar?' I asked. 'I always thought you were surrounded by dogs here.'

'While my father was alive, yes, we had so many dogs – you've seen the photos. I did keep a local dog after he passed away, which he would never have allowed. Only pedigree breeds for him.'

'I think of Jugaad often. Do you?' I asked. Lovely, sleek, four-legged child of ours. Jugaad was everyone's favourite on campus, but he clearly loved Akshar and me the most. We were his parents and that had made us a family, a strange, wobbly human-canine family.

'Yes, I do.' Akshar frowned. I wondered if he was thinking of Sahil's callous reference to Jugaad in the afternoon like I was. I hadn't met the younger brother in the mansion at all. It was as if he only existed outdoors.

'Shalini, you want a drink? G&T?' The question seemed to be a rhetorical one, he was already leaning backwards to press a switch on the wall behind him. In a matter of moments Ravinder was in the room, ready to grant Akshar his three wishes. He asked for whisky, ice cubes, gin, tonic water, lime slices, chicken cutlets and prawn chips. After Ravinder left, he put his arms behind his head and shut his eyes.

I went back to Maupassant, and Mathilde's singular crime of wishing she had been born an aristocrat. I glanced at the semi-horizontal aristocrat in the armchair, whose charms were wearing thin as far as I was concerned. Mathilde's story with its in-your-face moral undertones didn't appeal to me either.

It was early evening yet. I shut the book and my eyes, too. I needed to recoup my energies. I was looking forward to the gin and tonic more than anything

It was an unnaturally cold night for March, even for the hills. The gin and whisky kept us going but after a while Akshar asked Ravinder to fetch us blankets too. Akshar didn't need to lift a finger. Nor did I for these four days. Apart from Ravinder, there was his wife Savita who had tidied my room and made the beds. There was a young boy who ran errands for Ravinder and did the dusting, washed our clothes and ironed them. Then there was the fantastic chef who conjured up delicacies in a trice.

The conversation for the last hour had been determinedly pleasant. We talked about Jugaad, our school friends, Akshar's father – all that had been good in our lives.

We didn't count our drinks. I felt myself thawing. The afternoon fire seemed like a hazy thing of the past already. I could see that Akshar was not throwing back his drinks as fast as me, the level of single malt wasn't sinking like the gin.

'There's something I need to ask of you, Shalini, a favour,' he said when there was a pause in the conversation. He was looking into his glass and moving it slowly so the whisky see-sawed around in smooth, symmetrical waves.

'Ask away.' I hadn't seen this coming and it was foolish that I hadn't. Of course Akshar hadn't asked me to come all the way from Delhi because he was dying; he could as easily have died without bidding farewell to me.

'Let me make my request first and then you can ask me anything.'

'That sounds so formal and scary, Akshar. Ask quickly – I can't bear the suspense.' I was hurting somewhere inside – I knew whatever was coming, it would have nothing to do with me as a person, just a concrete material favour he needed.

He laughed. 'It's a simple request. I have set up a trust. What is called a private revocable trust. And I want you to be the trustee. In a nutshell, that's all.'

I narrowed my eyes, took a long gulp of gin and tonic and asked, 'And outside of the nutshell what does it imply?'

Akshar smiled. 'You will be required to sign the deed of trust, along with me. If you agree, I will ask my lawyer to come with the papers tomorrow morning and we can sign.'

Nicely done, I wanted to say. 'If you agree, I will ask' was hogwash; Akshar had already asked his lawyer to come, the papers were ready and I would be signing them. Neatly planned. I arrived yesterday, today I met Aahana, tomorrow I would sign and the day after I would leave.

'I'm not getting it … why do you need *me* to be the trustee? What is the trust for?'

'It's a trust whereby I leave everything I have, including this house and all other property I own, to Aahana's baby. They will inherit it when they turn eighteen. Till then Aahana will be what is legally called the beneficiary.'

'Oh,' I said uncomprehendingly. 'But why call me all the way from Delhi for this? Couldn't you have got someone you know in this town to sign?'

'I could have but it would have led to unnecessary gossip. And I wanted it to be the person I trust most in the world. So it had to be you,' Akshar said. He was speaking the truth, not trying to flatter me. Nor was I flattered. Trustee to Akshar's will. I had come all this way to sign a paper. Anyway, what had I expected.

'What's the matter?' Akshar was looking at me keenly.

'Nothing, just thinking …' I said. 'I feel you should have told me why you wanted me to come.' I didn't even understand it myself, the hold Akshar had over me. I knew every pore of his selfish being so well, yet every time there was this indescribable hurt.

'I didn't feel like talking about it on the phone,' Akshar dismissed me. 'Do you have any questions regarding how this will work?'

'Not right now – I'll ask if I think of anything.'

'So I'll tell Rana Mahajan, the lawyer, to come tomorrow by noon.'

'Yes, alright. But what will happen to Sahil if you leave everything to Aahana's baby?'

'There must be a reason my dad willed the house to me and almost all he owned.' Akshar narrowed his eyes; he didn't like the question.

'I'll go to bed now,' I said, suddenly feeling inordinately tired. I didn't really care what happened to Sahil. It wasn't late, just 9:30 p.m., but my mind and body were shutting down. I remembered the heat from the afternoon fire on my skin again. The fire, the visions.

'Oh, but dinner must have been laid. Eat a little and then we can go to bed?' Akshar asked.

'I'm quite full from the snacks,' I said. 'I'll see you in the morning, Akshar.'

He gave me a tentative hug and bid me goodnight. I wanted the hug to linger, to mean a little more. I wondered fleetingly how it would feel to kiss Akshar after all these years. He was my first kiss after all. I had decided back then, besotted that I was, that he was the world's best kisser. God knows he must have had more practice at it than the average fifteen-year-old.

One more night after this one.

I didn't even know what to expect – did trustees play a role in the beneficiary's upbringing? I really needed to stop being Akshar's eternal pushover. I decided I should at least have some questions ready for the lawyer. Anyway, the baby had parents – the Qureshis. I was just an external object meant to ensure the kid will get rich, or richer, as the case may be. That was hopefully the extent of my role.

Though I was in bed by 10 p.m., it took me a long time to fall asleep. I woke up just as I was drifting off to what seemed like the sound of footsteps outside the room. Soft, slow footsteps. I sat up in bed, my heart thumping. The silence in the hills is deeper and more resonant than elsewhere. Even the quietest of sounds can be disturbing.

Sahil stayed on the ground floor as far as I could remember. I reminded myself to ask Akshar the next day. But he could have come upstairs for some reason or the other. I would have expected Sahil to have quick, firm steps. The idea of him creeping stealthily down the corridor, slow, soft ... I don't know, I felt rattled.

But the silence was supreme now. Perhaps the muddle of half-sleep had confused me into imagining footsteps outside the door. I lay down again. The quilt acted as a security blanket, lulling me back to sleep.

When I woke up it was with this odd sensation of relief and foreboding rolled into one. Relief at the sunshine pouring in through the window. And relief that by this time tomorrow I would have left this mansion. Foreboding about the impending meeting with the lawyer. And foreboding as I remembered waking up to the sound of footsteps last night. I felt a chill pass through me. I lay in bed for a while, staring out of the window, messaging Mukul desultorily. I saw a couple of messages from my mother and replied to those as well, for a change. The fire in town hadn't made it to the national news or they would have asked anxious questions for sure.

I had dreamt of fire last night. It was natural after what I'd experienced in the morning. But Akshar hadn't been there in those dreams. Just women, a whole lot of them. I could remember one in which the women were all lined up in threes, me in front, bravely walking into a fire. Some of the women were dressed like the locals I had seen in these parts – dark make-up, long dresses and bright turbans on their heads. Some were from older times; they led the way, like the queens and princesses who walked into fires committing *jauhar*, ambassadors of the submission and dominance around which women so often define their lives. But then we walked out of the fire, too, in the same disciplined line, laughing as we came out into a meadow of green grass but with no sky, just a cemented ceiling.

After breakfast we moved to a lawn which I hadn't visited till now. It was on the other side of the driveway but a flight of steps down, so not visible till one came to the top of the steps. It was a beautiful lawn, bright with flowers. I walked around inspecting the flowerbeds. There was a circular bed with yellow cosmos growing in bunches to the right. It looked like a bouquet, a gift for the lawn visitors. Most beautiful though was the Japanese lantern, my father's favourite – the red petals stretched out horizontally with a plump purple inverted tulip in the middle. The colours so rich, so vibrant.

There was a large circular table in the middle of the lawn with six chairs around it – ornate dark green wrought iron. On one side were a rusty decrepit swing set and slide.

'I don't remember playing on those but Aahana insists we used to, apparently till we were seven or so,' said Akshar. 'I fell off the top of the slide once and almost died. Had to be rushed to Dr Qureshi – Reyhan's father.'

I imagined an unconscious little Akshar being rushed to hospital and a weeping little Aahana accompanying him.

'I don't remember hearing this before. Surely you didn't almost die?' I asked. Akshar started replying, then stopped when he saw a man in a crisp white shirt and black trousers coming down the stairs, carrying a set of files. He stood up and walked towards the man.

'Rana, hello,' he said, warmly, shaking the man's hand vigorously. He turned towards me. 'Meet my friend, Shalini. Shalini, this is Rana Mahajan, my lawyer and friend.'

We shook hands and Rana smiled a big gummy smile. He was tall, huge, with rosy childish cheeks. I liked him right away, which was a relief. I hadn't been looking forward to this meeting and a lawyer I didn't take to would have made it worse.

We exchanged the usual pleasantries before getting down to business. Delhi, weather, the insane goings-on in the world. Rana mentioned the fire on the mall road but neither Akshar nor I said we had been there.

'Everyone knows each other too well in this sort of a place, as you can imagine,' Rana replied to my question about growing up in a small town. 'There are deep bonds, an inter-dependence that is natural. Akshar of course is a recluse, but he knows we are all a phone call away.'

'And just growing up in the hills and all the beauty must be such a heavenly experience,' I said politely. Who knew what lay beneath, but we needn't go there.

'Our childhoods were idyllic in that way,' Rana agreed. 'But let's not romanticize it. End of the day, it's all the same. Messed up lives … what say, Akshar?'

'Tell me about it!' Akshar laughed his trademark mirthless laugh. 'So will you tell Shalini a little about the trust, what it entails for her as a trustee?'

'So, Shalini, it's really quite simple. Akshar is nominating you as a trustee to what we call his private revocable trust, and the beneficiary is Aahana's unborn child. The trust deed will be signed by the settlor – in this case, Akshar, the person creating the trust – and the trustees.' Rana was holding up a document, the trust deed I supposed, and looking at me questioningly to see if I was following.

I nodded and asked, 'But what does it really mean in terms of responsibility? What do I have to do as a trustee?'

'Well, it really depends on the terms and conditions in the trust deed. In this case, Akshar has kept it quite simple. I am also a trustee, along with you, so a lot of the things I will be able to take care of – like ensuring the rent from the properties owned by Akshar, all his dividends, interests, flow into the trust fund.'

'Okay, that's great. I mean, that both of us are trustees. But what do I have to do? I mean, why am I needed at all?' I asked.

'Basically, the idea of there being a trustee is that he or she is there to manage the trust after the settlor, umm … dies.' Rana looked down as he said it, and in that moment I felt a huge sense of nothingness. In spite of all my misgivings in the past few days or even years really, how was I to understand a world that didn't have an Akshar in it?

'But as a layperson who doesn't understand much of this … how can I be of any help at all?' I spoke to stop myself from thinking.

'It's not difficult. It might sound like too much now, but you'll figure it out. The trust deed clearly delineates our roles and duties. And if I act in a way that is contrary to the document, you can accuse me of a breach of trust. But we'll come to that.'

'Shall we go through the document a little? Shalini will know exactly what it entails then,' said Akshar. He gave a wan, loving smile, knowing I was feeling lost at the idea of an Akshar-less world.

Rana meanwhile had moved on. He was rifling through the pile of documents and handed one copy to me and one to Akshar. 'Okay, let's go through this point by point. Stop me when you have a question, Shalini.'

I had to snap out of the overwhelming thought of Akshar's death and focus on the practical aspects of providing for the living, in this case a child who was still to be born. I had always known Akshar was wealthy but the list of properties and investments was longer than I could have imagined. I tried to focus on the details.

One of the clauses was the provision of a salary for me – a higher amount of money per month than what I earned presently. I had assumed that to oversee this trust or make periodic checks into whether it was functioning properly was going to be a thankless, unpaid job. But the idea of earning a monthly salary after Akshar's death for the next eighteen years or so completely threw me.

'Akshar, this is crazy, I don't want this random salary or whatever.' I was appalled the more I thought about it, the idea of making money out of this felt preposterous.

'No, Shalini, sweetheart.' Akshar took me back fifteen years by saying that and I fought hard to stop myself from bursting into tears. 'I insist on this. I would have left you something anyway – and I know "salary" sounds weird but I want you to have this, I want you to know that even if I've always taken you for granted it doesn't mean I don't realize it. I'm just … too selfish to do anything about it.'

And then I was bawling. Akshar came and sat on the arm of my chair and held me and comforted me, his eyes glistening with tears he didn't know how to shed. Rana was clearly embarrassed; with renewed interest, he started going through the papers in front of him. Looking at him helped. I gulped, wiped my tears with my sleeves, then glanced at Akshar and suddenly we were both laughing.

Rana continued as if there had been no outburst. The document was long and though I was focusing the best I could, it was taking longer than I'd expected. Ravinder came out with drinks and snacks at some point. I wasn't hungry at all but took a can of Hoegaarden just because it was my favourite beer and Akshar had remembered. Ravinder gave me a sly sideways glance. He had one grey eye and one brown, a detail which made me uncomfortable once I noticed it. From the time I had arrived I had sensed that he disapproved of me. Same as the driver, Jai Singh. I had no idea why.

Rana and Akshar took beers too and helped themselves to the carrot sticks and asparagus and chips. Rana was relentless. He munched away with relish, speaking with his mouth full of food. I tried to focus on the words coming out rather than the food swirling around mushily inside.

By and large it wasn't difficult once I got used to the legalese. He was doing a good job. Not reading everything aloud but the few relevant lines of every clause, and then explaining if I wanted him to.

'I would like you to read it properly later and come back with questions if you have any,' he said. We exchanged phone numbers – bound together as co-trustees of Aahana's child's future.

Rana was on the last page of the document when he read out a clause that I couldn't fully grasp. It stated that the present house that Akshar stayed in would go to Aahana's child when they were eighteen or after Akshar's mother passed, depending on which happened first. Akshar's mother was already no more, what did that mean?

'And that is more or less all there is, Shalini,' Rana said briskly, while I sat numbly trying to make sense of the last clause he had mentioned. 'Can we sign? Though as I said, you can come back with questions as required and we will be in touch.'

I knew I was being rushed by both Rana and Akshar, like this was a distasteful task we needed to quickly airbrush and shove out-of-sight. It's also true that in the circumstances, in the face of death, any questions I might have had receded into meaninglessness. We signed ceremoniously, mournfully, on three originals of the document which would stay with each of us. Rana gathered them up when we were done. 'I'll get them registered and get some photocopies done as well.'

'You can courier Shalini's copy to her, Rana. She is leaving tomorrow morning,' Akshar said.

'Of course, of course.' Rana stood up. He glanced at his watch and looked a little alarmed. We had taken longer than I'd expected too. 'I really have to go. It was lovely meeting you, Shalini. And we'll be in touch.'

We shook hands. I leaned forward in my chair without getting up. 'Yes, lovely meeting you, Rana. Thank you for explaining it all so patiently and well.'

Akshar went halfway up the stairs with him and when he returned, he sat in the chair next to me. 'It seems so final suddenly. The ending.'

'But Akshar,' I said, no longer feeling emotional or maudlin, 'what was that about your mother? In the last clause.'

'I was wondering why you never asked about her,' he replied.

'What would I ask?'

'You know, just where she is or something.'

'What?' I was bewildered. 'Isn't she dead?'

'Who told you that?' He looked puzzled.

'What's wrong with you? You did. I probably still have the messages.' I was finding it difficult to breathe. I remembered reading the messages, how unsettled I'd felt.

'Don't be ridiculous. Show me.' Akshar looked displeased. I was already scrolling furiously through my messages. We didn't chat that often anymore so they weren't difficult to find, though it was six or seven months back.

'Here,' I said, handing him my phone. The first message from me was, How's your mother doing? His reply, Oh she's gone. My reply, I am so very sorry Akshar. And then his damning, Good riddance.

Akshar started laughing. 'God, Shalini, you do jump to conclusions, don't you? I told you she has dementia earlier, didn't I? All I meant was she is too far gone in the disease. There is not much trace of the person she was – so good riddance, as far as I'm concerned.'

'Oh …' I was trying and failing to process what he had said. In my head Akshar's mother had been dead for the last many months. 'I knew you never got along, so I didn't ask you anything the last two days.'

'That's fine. We didn't,' Akshar said. 'Let's go for lunch?'

'Akshar, where is she now? Your mother.' I felt a sense of dread flood my being as I asked this.

'Oh, she's on your floor. The other end, so you probably haven't seen the nurse going in and out. She hardly steps out anyway.'

'I … Akshar, even if she is … I mean, can I meet her?' This was all too strange. Just the idea that there was another whole person, and a nurse, tucked away in this bizarre mansion and I hadn't even realized it for the last few days.

'Yes, you can meet her. I can take you after lunch,' Akshar replied. 'I go to her room rarely – once or twice in a month.'

'Where is Sahil's room?' I remembered the soft footsteps from last night.

'On the ground floor.'

'Does he get along with your mother?' I asked.

He shrugged. 'They were always close. I don't know how often he visits her now.'

Akshar got up to go to the dining room and I followed him up the stairs slowly, my mind racing in so many directions. When we reached the driveway, I looked up at the second floor. One small window at the very end was open. It was impossible to tell from here if anyone was in the room but a bar of sunlight was playing on the half-drawn curtains, as if to inform those who wanted to know that there was a person inside the darkness.

5

the woman in the room

She looked out of the window and saw two men and a woman sitting in the sunken garden on the other side of the driveway. The woman wished she could be out there, the green beneath her feet, the sun in her eyes. And that cerulean nothingness above – there was a small word for it which she couldn't remember. It was all open and free, that blueness dotted with white powder puffs, not barred and imprisoned. And the cosmos. She had planted it. She could remember the names of many of the flowers in the garden while most everyday words had disappeared into a fog inside her head. That giant contraption – stairs on one side and all smooth on the other – down which her son had come, saying 'wheee', when he was a tiny boy. She didn't know why but it used to annoy her to hear him say 'wheee' – the animal-ness of a sound without meaning, the ridiculous childishness of that excitement. The older son.

The woman in the room did think of her older son occasionally. Perhaps he had died? Or maybe he was around. She couldn't quite remember. Her younger son, Sahil, born many years later when she so desperately needed someone who belonged to her, was here now. He visited her every day. She hadn't really wanted children. But that was inconceivable back in the day. Women, it was universally agreed, were born to be mothers, to create, to nurture. But Disha Gupta had been so alone, so lost, how could anyone have expected her to care for the scrawny mess that was her baby, her firstborn, the thing that was constantly thrust at her, that bawled and pooped and peed relentlessly. She had done what she could but when her mother-in-law cooed over the child and said how blessed they were she didn't quite understand why; all she had known was that she was sleep-deprived, unwell and more alone than she'd ever been.

It didn't improve as the boy grew bigger. What was she supposed to enjoy about this tiny person who cried and shouted when she didn't pay attention to him? There were moments when she had felt tender, a sense of wonder that this pretty child had come out of her body; there were moments when she had sensed how fragile he was and comforted him. But those moments never stayed. They slipped away and she had been left all alone again.

One day when he was six, she was on the terrace outside her bedroom, painting. A big easel in front of her and the glorious blue-grey hills beyond. Paints and brushes and water on a stool near her feet. A rare afternoon when she had felt at peace, when earth and nature and her own self came together so harmoniously that the dark weight that sat on her chest all the time had lifted and disappeared. When Akshar had come out and sat next to her and recited his nursery rhymes she had felt delight in the stuttering sweetness of his voice, kissed his apple-red cheeks and he, not very used to affection from his mother, had put his arms round her neck and hugged her tight.

After a while though, she had been drawn into the world of her painting again, of a boy with green hair and sad orange eyes, who both looked like Akshar and didn't. Akshar, bored, had tried to get his mother's attention by tugging at her right leg. The woman, taken by surprise, had lost her balance and toppled the canvas. It was all a muddle – paint, water, the canvas lying flat on its face on the ground. She had never shouted at her son or punished him in any way but her body would go rigid, her eyes cold, and that was always enough to make the child recoil. He would start crying and she would pretend he wasn't there. She had cleaned up and gone into her room. He had followed her, weeping, but she had said nothing, just laid down on her bed and shut her eyes.

Sahil was redemption. An accident she never regretted.

'I never managed to love my older son,' the woman told the nurse on one of her 'on' days. The nurse had started categorizing the woman's days as 'on' and 'off'. Like a switch that went off without warning and determined the mood for the hour or even sometimes for the full day.

This is why he never visits you even though you live in the same house, thought the nurse. But she didn't say it out loud. The woman had a vile tongue when she got angry. Not that the nurse took her seriously. It seemed she had been a bad wife and mother but here she was now, paying for her sins. The virtuous nurse felt forgiving.

the woman who left

The girl came up to her mother carrying a blood-soaked panty. She was not that small anymore, maybe twelve years old. 'Here,' she said. 'And there's blood between my thighs as well.'

'Oh,' Vasundhara jumped up, mortified. 'I should have told you …'

'I know what it is. Just wondered if you have sanitary napkins?'

'Yes, yes,' said Vasundhara. It was still so fraught between them. It was only when the girl was away at school that Vasundhara felt at ease. There were times when she felt they were improving, that their relationship was mending, but then there would be a new episode, something to set them back again.

That summer, soon after the little girl got her period, their driver gave his notice. Vasundhara didn't try to stop him. She wondered if the whole neighbourhood knew what had happened.

Ram-ji had been working with Vasundhara for four years. She had hired him when she had moved into this neighbourhood – a fresh start, the fire that had happened when the girl was seven years old behind them. They got along well, chatted desultorily on long drives about politics and Ram-ji's family. On that particular day she had been stuck in a meeting that went on longer than expected so when she got home, it was 8 p.m. already. She went to her bedroom to change while Ram-ji went to the kitchen to fill his old plastic Coca-Cola bottle with drinking water before going home.

As Vasundhara came out of her bedroom, she sensed that something was wrong. It was always like that. She would be filled with dread all of a sudden, like a premonition, and seven times out of ten something would have happened or was about to happen.

She put on the light in the living room and flicked on the TV. The noise of the television was always comforting. The doorbell rang and she opened the door to find Ram-ji standing outside.

'You haven't left yet?' she began, before noticing how agitated he was.

'Madam,' he said. 'Madam.'

In halting sentences, Ram-ji told Vasundhara what had happened. She asked him to come inside but he refused. He said he had filled his bottle and turned to leave the kitchen when Baby-ji (what he called the girl) had come into the kitchen. She was naked. And when he had taken a step backwards, she asked him what was the matter, smiled and came closer. He said he had pushed her in his hurry to get away. She had stumbled and he hadn't looked back.

'I don't know what she will tell you. She behaves strangely with me … sometimes … but today, today it was too much. I don't know if you believe me,' he said, anger and fear making him stammer.

Vasundhara felt shame flood her every sense. How could she tell him that she believed him right away? No mother would do that, would they? The man, she could see, was scared for his life, for what the little girl was going to tell her mother. He knew he didn't have a chance. A forty-year-old man and a twelve-year-old girl who was tall for her age with budding breasts and a body that was developing too fast.

When Vasundhara went to the girl's bedroom she was sitting at her study table, wearing shorts and a t-shirt, scribbling something in a notebook.

'Did you go to the kitchen when Ram-ji was filling water?' Vasundhara asked, wishing her voice wasn't so high-pitched and nervous.

'Don't remember, maybe I did,' said the girl, drawling, careless.

'Were you …' Vasundhara couldn't say it. She looked into the girl's cold, beady eyes and couldn't say the word 'naked' – it got stuck somewhere in her throat and refused to come out. She coughed, as if to spit out the word, but it stayed where it was, inside her throat. The girl smiled, pushing her limp hair back from her face. The trademark smile that she reserved specially for her mother, her thin, dry lips tilting and forming a vacuous horizontal crescent moon. Her skin, which had gotten a healthier glow in the last few years, was looking pasty again; the tiny lump of heart-shaped flesh on her collarbone was throbbing.

The next day when Ram-ji said he wanted to leave the job Vasundhara nodded mutely. She paid him the salary that was owed to him and wondered if she should offer to pay more. He would have to look for a new job, and she knew he had a wife and two young children. But she couldn't afford to show how she felt, how she believed him and felt awful for him. She just wanted to put the whole incident behind them. She didn't accuse him of anything but just nodded and paid up and watched him leave from the window.

Ram-ji got on his moped. He seemed to have aged overnight. Unsure of what had happened, yet tense and fearful. Vasundhara watched him fade into the distance, a lost figure hunched over the handles of his moped. She wished him well. She consoled herself by thinking that drivers were much in demand, and he would get a job easily.

the woman who was unafraid of fire

Lunch was a silent affair. Akshar and I didn't speak much, sunk into our own worlds and thoughts which sometimes overlapped, sometimes didn't. I was almost happy when Sahil came slouching into the room.

'One more fire,' he said. 'Lower down, halfway to the plains.'

I shook my head. I had a train to catch the next morning. The situation seemed to be deteriorating by the hour.

'The local women are initiating measures – roads are being sprinked with ice chips, and they are pruning the trees and bushes.'

'Why? Is that supposed to help?' I was surprised.

'It's a ritual calming of the earth; they believe environmental excesses are causing the fires,' Sahil said. 'I heard they are going to demand all factories be shut down, and that the industrialists take some steps, Akshar.'

I looked at Akshar, who shrugged. 'Let them talk to the lobbies. I am happy to cooperate if their demands are reasonable.'

Sahil laughed and said to me, 'Akshar always cooperates when the women make demands.'

'How come it's only the women who are bothered about the environment?' I countered.

'It is what it is,' muttered Akshar, not wanting to be drawn in. 'Who the fuck knows what's going on. Anyway, Shalini, let's go and meet my mother since you said you want to.'

'Yes, please, I'd like to,' I said.

Sahil laughed; not a pleasant laugh, but forced and high-pitched. 'Mom is lucky – Akshar is going to visit her. Wow.'

'You don't live here, Sahil; I am the one that pays her bills and looks after her,' Akshar said coldly.

'Looks after her … you do, do you? Good little Mama's boy.'

Akshar didn't look at him as he got up. 'Come, Shalini,' he said and left the room without checking if I was coming or not.

I glanced at Sahil, and he shrugged, 'Leave while you can. Curfews are going to be imposed. No one wants tourists; they're a liability – hotels and restaurants are going to shut down for a couple of weeks I've heard.'

'I am leaving tomorrow.' He didn't have to tell me to leave.

'Just saying. I bumped into Dr Qureshi, Aahana's …' Sahil winked at me. It was distasteful. I gave him a cold stare. 'Anyway, he said hospital staff and the local women who have gathered at the hospitals are getting special training on how to deal with burn victims. He seemed nervous.'

'Are you coming, Shalini?' Akshar's impatient shout echoed from the corridor. Sahil smirked as I left the room quickly.

When Akshar and I reached the top floor we turned left, my room was down the corridor to the right. We went past a couple of rooms, they were bolted and not used at all from the look of it. Akshar knocked and turned the handle to open the door at the end of the hall.

We entered a large and lofty room much like the one I was staying in but the solitary window behind the bed was very narrow, so sunlight didn't flood the room like it did mine – just a few beams of light here and there giving an overall impression of dinginess. And there was no pretty rug or bedsheet either; it was a drab room with peeling plaster. Whitewashing it seemed was done selectively in this mansion.

The carved black four-poster bed in the centre of the room was grand though. Sitting erect in the middle of it was a gaunt woman with a long torso in a shapeless nightgown and thick long grey hair streaming over her shoulders and down her back. Beside her, two side tables laden with medicines and photos in dull silver frames and a couple of books. In one corner was a lumpy sofa on which sat a nurse in a white uniform – a peaked cap, socks and black polished shoes, stitching something on a piece of yellow cloth.

The nurse got up and Akshar nodded at her. Next to the bed were two chairs. Akshar sat in one and I sat in the other. Akshar's mother had not moved at all but her eyes were darting here and there, at us and then around the room. Her lips were moving a little, she gave a deep sigh, then spoke in a voice that was surprisingly loud and contrasted with the stillness of her posture.

'It's the petunias – they just won't bloom. But never mind. Let it be. None of them have ever behaved well, have they?'

I leaned forward in my chair, and she fixed her eyes on me and smiled. It was an unexpectedly sweet smile.

'I like you. You are a good girl.' Her eyes darted to Akshar and she gave him a cunning look. When she looked at me again, her voice dropped to a whisper.

'That other one though. Ruined his life, she did. Took away everything, everything.'

'What bullshit are you speaking?' Akshar demanded.

'He knows.' Her eyes were fixed on me. She didn't look at him at all. 'Avyukt knows everything, and so does his son.'

'I'm leaving.' Akshar stood up. His cheeks were flushed, and his eyes and lips were enraged slits.

'Don't be angry, don't be angry,' she said, sliding off the bed and going to where there was a switchboard with three switches. She started fumbling with them. 'You want to listen to Humpty Dumpty? Or a song?'

'God the amount of bullshit she can spout.' Akshar shook his head, looking more defeated than angry now. 'You can tell why I don't want to come here and visit her, Shalini, can't you?'

'I really don't know, Akshar,' I said. 'It's just very sad ...'

The flimsy strands of logic within the unreason of her speech must have been the hardest for Akshar to accept. Who had ruined their lives? Aahana, I supposed. But as the woman tried to pacify Akshar with nursery rhymes, as she may have done when he was a baby, there was something unbearably tender in that moment.

'It would be sad if she had ever been present in my life, been the mother I wanted, needed,' Akshar said, angrily. In the meantime, his mother was wandering round the room, her hands restless. She stopped by one of the side tables, picked up a hairbrush and put it in her mouth.

'Now, now, give that to me,' the nurse was by her side in a trice. 'What all you do. Does that look like food to you? Like a chocolate?'

Akshar's mother laughed, a light girlish giggle. 'I want chocolate. Give?' She held out her hand almost pleadingly.

'Oh, does she like eating chocolates?' I asked the nurse.

'She loves it. But it's not good for her teeth and she is forgetting how to brush. Swallows the toothpaste and water when I brush her teeth. So difficult.'

I went up to Akshar's mother and put my hand on her shoulder. 'You do that?' I asked, smiling. 'I'll get chocolates for you if you promise to brush your teeth properly.'

She looked at me with eager eyes and said, like a child, 'Yes, promise.' And then added, 'My son has gone to school now. He is a good boy. Don't say anything to him.'

I looked at Akshar. The expression on his face was inscrutable. I understood his childhood grievances. Of an uncaring mother, a mother who didn't get along with his father or grandmother and who didn't like his girlfriend, who was unhappy and bored and drank too much and smoked and scandalized the neighbours.

'It's early onset, Akshar?' I asked. I was familiar with Alzheimer's because of my grandmother but then she was eighty when she got it, not in her fifties as must have been the case with Akshar's mother.

'Yes,' Akshar said. 'The decline has been rapid. And hard.'

Akshar's mother had drifted back to where we were. She was sitting on one corner of the bed now and looking at me intently.

'You stay,' she said. 'Send the other one away.'

'Mama, can you stop this?' Akshar said. She started giggling and covered her mouth with one hand.

'Going to have a baby now,' she said to me. 'Big stomach.'

Akshar and I exchanged surprised glances. He looked at the nurse, who was shuffling her feet and looking embarrassed. 'Oh, she just says things … sometimes she looks down from the window and watches, you know.'

'Is my mother going to come today? Let me check.' Akshar's mother got up again and peered out of the window, as if on command. 'I don't see her. I don't see the *chudail* also. With her big stomach.'

That was when Akshar lost it. He strode towards the window and started shouting.

'All my life. All my life! You can't let me be, can you? Even now, when your mind is gone, still. What sort of a woman are you who can't bear to see her own son happy?'

His mother looked bewildered. She held on to the bars of the window and started rocking back and forth. I went up and shook Akshar's arm.

'Stop it. Let's go,' I said. I held Akshar's arm and led him away towards the door. I threw a pleading look at the nurse as we left and was glad to see she was already at Akshar's mother's side, rubbing her left arm up and down comfortingly.

'This is why I don't go to see her. She is out of her mind but still a vindictive old bitch. You heard her, Shalini, she is insane!' Akshar was still shouting as we walked down the corridor.

'It's okay. She doesn't know what she's saying – it's just old thoughts that are resurfacing in strange ways – she can't help it,' I said as soothingly as I could. What I couldn't tell him was the immediate sense of connection I had felt with his mother. A sense of coming home. I shivered. I had never felt this way with anyone before.

'She has always been like this. Why can't you understand, Shalini? She has never been a kind person. Never been a good mother.' He was mad at me too now. 'I don't know why you are suddenly overflowing with love for her. Why did you even want to meet her? And I stupidly went with you. Usually I just go in for a minute or two, just to check on the nurse. But give her a chance, even now when she's mad as a hatter, she rips into you.'

I kept quiet. I had nothing to say. She was his mother. Tucked away like a madwoman, like a gender archetype, like the woman in *The Yellow Wallpaper*. It's as if her life wasn't real, she's alive within the pages of a novel or a film. Novels, the distorted versions of reality that they are, bristled with the excesses of women who didn't have a safe space for their so-called insanities. Perhaps that would be how I lived the last years of my life too. Who knew?

'Jai Singh knows he has to take me to the railway station tomorrow morning, right?' I asked Akshar to change the subject.

'Oh, you can't wait to leave, can you?' he replied nastily. 'Go running back to your perfect life and amazing new boyfriend.'

'That's not fair, Akshar, but I'll let it go.'

'As always. Always the martyr. Bearing the brunt of my rages.'

'Yes, that's quite accurate actually.' I was suddenly very angry. 'Stupid me.'

Akshar didn't reply. We were on the landing between the second and first floors.

'Look, Akshar, I'm going to go and pack. I'll come down in an hour if you want me to.' I didn't wait for his reply but turned, went up the flight of stairs and into my room.

Packing calmed me. I folded my clothes neatly and put them in the suitcase. What I would wear in the morning I put on a hanger in the big oak cupboard, which smelt of mothballs and dust. I put my laptop on charge so I could use it in the train if I felt like it. Savita knocked at the door and came in with a cup of tea and some freshly baked peanut cookies at 5 p.m.

I dragged a chair to the window so I could watch the sun set. Mukul called. I took the call but felt too empty to speak. He had read about the fire on the mall road and was agitated. I wondered what he would say if I told him I had almost been consumed by that very same fire.

'You need to get back soon, Shalini.' I was not sure why he felt the need to say this, knowing I was returning the next day. Perhaps a misplaced sense of ownership where I was concerned.

I felt a sudden burst of anger, of the sort I had learnt to control over the years. My hands started trembling and I disconnected the call. Mukul didn't call back. Good. I tried to calm down using the exercises my therapist – the only one out of the ten I had been to that I had connected with – had taught me. If I was in a good place today it was because of her.

I saw a couple of messages from Akshar. Come down soon – I am chilling us a bottle of wine. He was trying to be amicable, as had always been the case when he felt slightly stupid after a temper tantrum. I smiled a little, I felt better.

I made my way slowly down the stairs. Akshar had shouted at me the way he had so often when we were young. How could I take it to heart? These could be our last few hours together in this lifetime. He was waiting for me in the TV room, looking so frail and lost. I made my way into his arms like a tributary that flows into a river without thought. He held me tight and I, overwhelmed and lost, broke down – I was weeping into his shoulder and I could feel his bony body tremble as he tried to control himself. As I held him, I felt a sliver of desire pass through my body; a residual lust that refused to go away despite all that had happened. It shamed me, my failure at self-respect where Akshar was concerned.

I had questions, but I didn't care for the answers anymore. I would let them go. Drinks and snacks were laid out on a trolley. 'How often do you drink, Akshar?' I asked, taking a tissue from the trolley and blowing my nose rather vigorously into it.

'Once a week usually,' he replied. 'But never more than a couple of drinks. My health doesn't really allow it.'

The TV was on mute. We chatted desultorily, both of us tired and drained, my heart in a thousand pieces. At 8 p.m., Akshar got a call from Aahana asking him to switch on the television. I wished she would leave us alone on my last evening.

On the news channel, a nationwide lockdown was being announced, which would come into effect in four hours. Trains, aeroplanes, cars – no movement would be permitted from midnight onwards, for twenty-one days. Just like that. Out of the blue with no warning. There were no instructions on how citizens should go about taking care of their day-to-day needs – food, medicines, money, travel – there would be a complete lockdown with no compromises. The result was immediate panic and confusion. Messages flooded my phone. Mukul called.

'What are you going to do?' he asked. 'You won't be able to take the train tomorrow.'

I felt like my head was in a fog. I asked dumbly, 'I don't know. What will I do?'

Mukul replied, 'I don't know.'

There was a knock at the door. It was Ravinder. He said Jai Singh was asking about the next morning – would I be going to the railway station? I wondered if the two men were gloating at the idea of my plans being in disarray.

'No, madam will be staying with us till the lockdown lifts,' Akshar said peremptorily, without looking at me.

'But …' I said. And shut up.

'He could take you to the railway station – I could organize that. But trains won't be running. And state borders will be sealed, so he can't drive you to Delhi,' Akshar said. I nodded. He and Ravinder had a short conversation about provisions and groceries while I tried to collect my thoughts. Akshar seemed to have taken the news in his stride. In any case, he stayed alone in his castle like an incarcerated princess. Lockdown wouldn't make much of a difference to him.

This was Akshar. I could stay a few extra days with him. It was nothing. Akshar was my whole childhood, the building block on which I painstakingly constructed my childhood and even my adult life. But that sense of foreboding returned – the way I'd felt on the first day when I entered this mansion. A sense of something eerie and wrong. I would be walking these dingy corridors for three more weeks.

A huge mansion with twenty rooms and three humans? If I counted myself and the nurse, five – not too bad. And the domestic staff in the outhouse. How grand. How dismal.

'What are you thinking?' asked Akshar.

I was about to say '*The Shining*' but stopped myself in time. I could feel nervous laughter bubbling inside me. I remembered how Akshar's mother had covered her mouth and giggled in the afternoon. The laughter inside me died. I remembered the mall road. Akshar calling me from somewhere deep inside the fire, the visions, mesmeric, enchanting. I rubbed my temples with my index fingers as if I had a headache.

'I'm just worrying about the logistics … work …' I said to Akshar who was still looking at me enquiringly. I couldn't tell him how panicked I was feeling.

'There's a lockdown. Nothing's going to happen. Your office will be shut anyway. You can work from here like you would have from home.'

Akshar still found it hard to imagine that I had a life outside of him. After ten years in which we had met only a handful of times he still assumed I could never yearn for another life when I was with him. That other life, whatever it was, was irrelevant.

My phone rang again. This time it was my dad. I told him I was going to be stuck there for a while. I had the exact same conversation with my mother when she called too, five minutes later. She sounded more worried than my father had, probably because she disapproved of Akshar, compounded by the fact that she very much approved of Mukul, whom she had met a couple of times.

'You are really connected to your parents now,' Akshar said when I finished speaking to them. 'Not surprised about your dad, but your mom too!'

'Well, she wasn't doing that great last year and that made me think ...' I paused. I couldn't quite explain without being melodramatic. Ma had undergone a hysterectomy. Seeing her, frail and thin between the hospital sheets, had changed something within me. 'I'm not a kid anymore. I no longer blame her for ... for anything, really.' My voice was sharper than I intended it to be. What had I blamed her for? I couldn't even remember. Just that life had got better once I let go of the hatred, to a certain extent. I never would be able to let go of it completely.

'There are so many things I still need to tell you, Shalini,' Akshar said, diverting the conversation back towards himself.

'Tomorrow maybe? We have more time to catch up than we expected,' I offered.

I wanted to go to my room and speak to Mukul once more. The idea of a nation coming to a grinding halt, of being stuck because of a travel ban and trains not running was absurd. But three weeks aren't all that long. Three weeks with Akshar, my first love. My only love? No, I didn't want to go there. I could not.

This time, I was sure. I was tossing and turning in bed, sleep far away, when I heard them. Soft, padded footsteps. Past my door and then after some minutes, once more … slow and deliberate … as if the person was returning after reaching the end of the corridor. Sahil was on the ground floor so it couldn't be him. Or could it? I felt my throat drying up. There was a jug of water and a glass on the side table, but I couldn't will myself to sit up, pour a glass and drink. I could only huddle under the covers, my throat parched.

It could be the nurse, of course, taking a walk after her patient had fallen asleep for the night. I imagined the dingy, dimly lit corridor and the matronly nurse in starched white, walking up and down with stately, measured steps.

I managed to get some uneasy sleep but woke up early. Unlike the last couple of days, the room wasn't flooded with sunlight. A blue-black sheen sat lightly over everything, a skin of translucent light. I looked towards the window, at the rain-streaked sky. I shut my eyes and willed myself to fall asleep again to the sound of the liquid jingle-jangle of rain. I loved the rain, especially in summer when it came in fits and starts, to give overheated Delhi moments of respite. But in the hills I preferred sunlight – bright, cheerful, radiant – on the cold emerald slopes.

After a couple of hours, I made my way downstairs. The walls seemed moist and swollen, even deep inside the house. Akshar was sitting on the porch outside the dining room. I served myself some fruit, muesli with cold milk and joined him.

'Aahana is hysterical,' he said with no context, as if her behaviour had a self-evident logic that would be obvious to me. 'I can't function when she gets this way.'

'You haven't had breakfast?' I asked and he shook his head. I held out my plate and said, 'Have some chiku.'

Akshar didn't look at me or at the plate. He murmured instead, 'How will she cope when I'm gone ...'

I wanted to point out that they weren't together, that she had a husband. She would cope like she was doing now, except there would be no more Akshar Mondays in her calendar.

'She will have her baby,' I said, deliberately frivolous. 'And you've provided for the baby too, Akshar. Which is nice of you.'

I didn't quite know why I added 'nice of you' but it made Akshar stop scanning the distant hills, shimmering and heavy with rain. He turned to look at me. 'Nice of me? To provide for my baby?'

I stared at Akshar. I hadn't even suspected this. How naive was I? Despite the whole trust deed rigmarole, despite all the desperate love between Akshar and Aahana, the thought hadn't crossed my mind.

Akshar gave me a twisted smile. 'You're right in a way, I might have done this regardless – for Aahana's baby, no matter who the father was. But it's harder to leave the world knowing this baby is mine.'

All the questions that had built up in my head about the great Akshar–Aahana love story returned. I asked, without trying to weigh the words, 'Why is she married to Reyhan Qureshi then?'

'Aahana married Reyhan because it wasn't possible for her to marry me,' Akshar replied. 'Reyhan has been in love with her forever. And once she was pregnant – it was a mistake – she didn't want to abort. It seemed like marrying Reyhan was the best idea. This is a conservative little town. Hard to be a single mother here.'

It made no sense to me. The best idea was to marry someone else when she was in love with Akshar? 'Why wasn't it possible for her to marry you?'

'For one thing, I would lose my inheritance if we married. All of this would have gone to my father's nephew; all my investments, down to the last paisa, so to speak. My mother ensured that. Sahil has his share of Dad's inheritance, but it's insignificant, and anyway he will do what he wants with his own money. Besides, we don't know who Sahil's dad is. Dad didn't. Maybe Sahil does if Mama has told him.'

'Akshar, back up.' I was exasperated. 'Tell me properly or don't.'

'It's a long story,' Akshar sighed.

It was cold and miserable on the open porch. It wasn't the right atmosphere for what promised to be a protracted tale of love and betrayal, but I did want to hear it. 'Can we go to your study or something?'

We moved to Akshar's study and settled down. The story that Akshar told me was unreal – filled with anachronistic plot twists, a masala blockbuster of sorts. I didn't interrupt, I let him take his time.

It seemed Akshar's mother, Disha, had never liked Aahana. It was much later that the whole story would come out, but even when little Aahana and Akshar roamed the hills together, picking flowers and playing catch, his mother it seemed had been suspicious.

To begin with, Avyukt and Meher were secretly charmed by the great love that their children – unknowing siblings, both Avyukt's, one Meher's – shared. But as the two grew older, they slowly became aware, then alarmed, to find that Akshar and Aahana's love was not that of siblings. One summer afternoon, when they were twenty-one or -two, Meher had returned home early from work to find Aahana's bedroom door locked. Much scrambling ensued when she knocked, and it took a while for a furiously blushing Aahana to open the door. Over her shoulder Meher could see Akshar standing near the window, a silhouette that reminded her of Avyukt Gupta and horrified her.

That evening, Meher had called Avyukt and told him that the lovers needed to be separated. It's first love, they'll outgrow it, Avyukt had tried to reason, but Meher, shaken by what she had witnessed in the afternoon, insisted something had to be done.

Avuykt Gupta had thought about it. Incest was distasteful and unacceptable but he was an indulgent, loving father – how was he supposed to engineer this break-up without upsetting his beloved bratty son? He let a few days slide by. And then his wife had seen a text message from Meher flash on his phone, without quite intending to – she was seriously uninterested in her husband's affairs by this time. Avyukt, we have to do something about it. This can't continue. For crying out loud, it's incest.

Disha had known for some years now about Meher and Avyukt, though she had no idea when the affair had started. She hadn't guessed it had been going on for two decades, that Aahana was her husband's daughter. But the word incest jumped out at her and she knew. It was almost like she had always known. She had never thought of herself as an intuitive person but every time she had seen Aahana, her heart had clouded over in a manner she couldn't explain.

Disha hadn't confronted Avyukt, not right away. She had poured herself a whisky instead, she loved a good single malt. It was the fact that Aahana and Akshar shared a birthday that had bewildered her the most. She could remember the nurse holding out a newborn Akshar to her. She had looked up at Avyukt, who had his arm around her in that moment she had assumed was theirs alone, never mind how messed up their love and life became in the following years.

At the same time, in another room in the same nursing home, Meher had given birth to her daughter. Disha wondered if Avyukt had been torn, longing to be at her bedside too. Had Meher always known the child was Avyukt's?

Disha had poured herself another drink and sat by the window. One after another the jagged pieces of the puzzle came together till she wondered at her own naivete. Any guilt she had felt at Sahil's birth vanished.

And from the window she had seen Akshar and Aahana strolling across the lawn, chatting and laughing without a care in the world. Avyukt had taken such pleasure in their friendship. He was the ever-doting father; it made Akshar so happy, that his dad loved Aahana, almost as if she was his own daughter. Disha had laughed to herself at that thought, and felt so alone that she didn't know how to bear it.

A slow rage had built up inside her, as if she was a dark room and there was an old film unspooling inside her, toxic memories in black and white. From that moment it had all unravelled, and Akshar blamed his mother for it. For the way she had stormed into Avyukt's study, for the filthy abuse she had heaped on her husband, for the way so many hearts had broken that evening, the moment Akshar and Aahana realized they were siblings.

That evening Disha was consumed by hatred. The sight of her husband sitting with his head in his hands at his grand mahogany desk, Akshar and Aahana terrified and weeping, none of it had moved her. Instead she had picked up her phone, called Meher and said there was an emergency, so Aman and she must come over immediately. Aman's sorrow was deeper than Disha's. In that moment of revelation, he had been rendered childless. Erstwhile father and daughter had looked at each other, not knowing what to do with all the love that was there between them, that couldn't just lessen in a moment's knowledge. Aahana had stolen glances at Avyukt and Akshar – her brand-new father and brother – as years of deceit and cheating had peeled away like plaster. They were all each other's gaping wounds; the parents, the children.

In Disha's life the only source of grace that remained was Sahil, who was not her husband's son, as he had always guessed. Their lives were too separate and bitter by that time, fidelity a non-issue. But Disha had been ashamed, deeply ashamed, more than she had let on. It had been too late to abort by the time she had realized she was pregnant but then Sahil was born and she at least had one person that was her own, just hers.

Sahil was only ten that day when Disha had realized Aahana was Avyukt's child, away at boarding school. Perhaps if he had been in the house Disha wouldn't have behaved the way she did, getting drunk and summoning Meher and Aman, causing their lives to come to a sudden denouement; no foreplay, no slow building up of the narrative to soften the blows, all of it so shocking and horrible.

By the time Akshar's story came to an end the sun had shifted in the sky and the sunlight fell in a different pattern across the room which had witnessed the unravelling of the very same secrets ten years back. It intrigued me to think that this was where it had all happened, where Disha had gathered all the players on whom the story impinged and revealed all she had deducted from a single text. And here I was more than a decade later, hearing Akshar laying bare the very happenings that were buried in all the corners of this room.

What was weird to me was how Akshar's devotion to his father hadn't wavered even when he got to know the truth. His mother – the troubled alcoholic, the one who revealed all – was to blame, as if her utterance about the past had brought it all into being.

Perhaps he never got a chance to blame his father, maybe he would have if Avyukt Gupta hadn't that very night had a stroke that paralyzed the left side of his body.

That night, after Avyukt went to bed at 3 a.m., Disha had stayed up smoking in the terrace that adjoined their bedrooms. Akshar had paced the lawns outside. There was a moment when he had looked up at his mother and it had seemed to him that she was covered in flames and smoke, as she leaned on the squat railings that ran along the terrace. A trick of the eye perhaps, as the night sky had ceded to an orange dawn in the mist-covered mountains. His mother, all bones and elongated like a shadow – the window behind her full of light, as if on fire. The window of the room in which Avyukt Gupta had been sleeping.

Avyukt Gupta didn't get out of bed the next morning. When Akshar had gone to wake him up at noon, he was blubbering, his neck and mouth covered in snot and saliva, his eyes open and glassy. The doctor said he'd had a stroke that night. For the next six months he had lived on, shrivelled and damaged, his mind clear even as his body struggled. Until finally, one night, he had raved and ranted as his mind joined his body and both gave up at dawn.

Disha remained hard and inflexible through it all and as Avyukt withered in front of her eyes, she had made him draw up a will disinheriting Akshar if he ever married Aahana.

'Would you have married if that clause wasn't there in the will?' I asked.

'Perhaps not,' Akshar shrugged. 'But just the idea of my mom forcing him to do that … she was so exulting and vicious those last few months. My dad died a broken man. For the next seven or eight years, even after Dad died, Aahana and I were so lost; our relationship could never quite forego the patterns of love that we had set across the years, yet I think the idea of marrying each other – half-siblings that we are – wasn't something we considered.'

'You continued to have a sexual relationship?'

'Not at first, not for a long time. But slowly, yes, we came back to each other. We didn't know how not to. Obviously, though, the pregnancy was a mistake.'

Nothing was very obvious in this story to me. Akshar was pale in the light that streamed in from the window, his skin sallow, breathing heavy. He was drumming his fingertips on his desk, the sharp ticking sound made me think of the deathwatch beetle, bumping its head against the darkness of tunnel walls as it bored into decaying old wood.

6

the woman in the room

She was curious about the fires. She had heard the nurse talking about 'The Burnings' on the phone, the media moniker for the global crisis that had plunged the known world into chaos. Many years ago, as a schoolgirl she had read about the Great Fire of 1666 in London. She had been inordinately delighted by the fact that it had started on her birthday, 2 September, in a bakery. Every year since, she thought about the Great Fire when the candles on her cake were lit. She imagined the candles overturning – the table, the room, the city all lit up like a giant birthday cake just for her.

The Lord Mayor of London hadn't taken the fire seriously at first and said it was so weak that 'a woman could piss it out'. Such a comment would have made the fire angry. It would have sought vengeance.

'There are fires, and it's best you listen to the women.'

'What rubbish you speak,' said the nurse. It was perfectly true, the woman knew, but it was fine if the nurse didn't understand; she was pretty much a moron any which way.

'So yes,' she said, deciding to change the subject. 'When I burnt up as a child my mother gave me barley water to drink, and she put wet bandages on my forehead to make the fever go away.'

The nurse murmured, 'That's nice.'

'I want my mother. She can look after me. Is she in the other room?' The woman got off the bed and went towards the window. She confused doors and windows all the time. As the nurse had told her son the last weekend, it was lucky the bars were there, otherwise what if she climbed onto the sill and tried to leave the room through a window one day?

'That's the window. It's not a door.'

'But I can hear my mother calling.' The woman looked at her suspiciously. She could hear her mother calling her, loud and clear. She was asking her to come outside, it was a sunny day and she shouldn't stay cooped up in the house, always stuck to her drawing book. Disha Gupta went to the window and held the bars, tried to shake them. 'Why won't you let me go out?'

'There are fires out there. You can get burnt and die.' Today the nurse wasn't feeling entertained by the woman's inanities, sometimes they really got on her nerves.

'I am not scared of fires. You should be. Fires like me but they may not like you. Then what will you do?' the woman asked. The nurse rolled her eyes. Sometimes the woman threw a fit, got violent. She was still a physically strong person. The other day when they were in the bathroom, she wouldn't let the nurse clean her, just simply standing up after finishing her job. It was disgusting. On some days she would try to get out of the shower cubicle before the soap was washed off her body, struggle and push the nurse as she tried to finish bathing her.

'God knows I can't let her be unclean,' she told her friend Rita. 'But it's a battle sometimes. And her filthy tongue … though that I can ignore. She even tried to bite me the other day when I was feeding her.'

'Sounds horrible,' said Rita. 'You can leave, you know. Let her son find another nurse.'

The nurse sighed. It wasn't bad all the time, she had to admit, but it was a degenerative disease – things were only going to get worse.

'I was thinking I will ask for an assistant – it's getting difficult to manage on my own,' she said. 'The son isn't stingy. He just doesn't want to be bothered.'

The nurse prided herself on the way she functioned. It felt a little defeatist to ask for help. But it was lonely too. It would be good to have someone to speak to. When Ravinder's wife, Savita, came to clean the room every morning they chatted for a while.

Ravinder and Savita adored the older son, Akshar. The half-sister visited him every week but never came to see his mother. And why should she? She wasn't her mother. It was the town gossips who alleged she was Akshar's half-sister but the nurse, even after all these years of living in the mansion, didn't know if such an outlandish claim could be true. Regardless, she did know from Ravinder's wife that Disha Gupta, when she didn't have dementia, used to be rude and obnoxious with her son and had reduced Aahana to tears many times.

When Savita and the nurse chatted, the woman sat on the bed and rocked back and forth. The nurse knew that meant she was agitated, that she didn't like the cleaning woman.

'She hated me. No one in Avyukt's house liked me,' she said one day after Savita had swept and mopped the room, chatted with the nurse and left. 'Now she acts like I don't exist, and I don't. I am not here. I am away.'

The woman had a faraway look in her eyes. She was away. That was the only upside of dementia – it allowed her to be where she wanted. Though sometimes, her mind took her to places she wanted to forget. Then she shut her eyes tight, clenched her fists. But it was hard on those days, when the darker memories claimed her. Of a teenage son who hated her, of a string of lovers whom she had not loved. Whom had she ever loved? She didn't know. Her mother, in the desperate way that children did. Her husband, briefly. A man she had met at a bar in Delhi, spent one night with and never forgot till dementia took away his name but left her with the scent of a person who had given her an evening to remember. Her younger son she had loved the most; still did when she saw him, when she remembered who he was. It was enough, perhaps. Occasional tastes of love that sometimes wafted in the air, even today.

the woman who left

Vasundhara worried about her daughter. She wished she could be near her. A wish that arose from a lifetime of anxiety about her child, not maternal instinct. Of course not, it had never been that. She had long ago stopped trying to understand the nature of the attachment that tied her to her daughter. A desperate bond of hopelessness and responsibility and the fear of suddenly being summoned to her daughter's side. It had happened too many times. Some of those incidents she'd blocked so effectively that they no longer existed, like forgotten dreams. Some she went over and over again in her mind till they became powerless. Like the time she and Adil were vacationing in Thailand.

They had gone to Chiang Mai for a short break, leaving the little girl with her paternal grandmother. Vasundhara remembered how excited she had been, how heady it was to just be alone with Adil, away from the blank eyes of her own daughter, eyes that made her nervous – as if the child was always judging her, all the time, every time.

They were sitting poolside on lounge chairs, sipping martinis, watching the picture-book sunset, when Vasundhara had been informed by an attendant that she needed to call India. Pre-mobile phone times, when nothing was a quick call away.

Her daughter couldn't be found. The grandmother had been hysterical; her son was already on his way from Singapore where he now lived with his new wife.

Her voice had been heavy with accusation as she told her daughter-in-law of yore that her son had told her not to call Vasundhara, to let her enjoy her break, but she couldn't, could she? As a mother she had to know, right?

Vasundhara had held the phone to her ear, the euphoria of the last two days ebbing away, the customary dread that her daughter induced returning. They were scheduled to go back the next day, anyway. Her ex-husband had told her not to change the flight, that he was on his way to Delhi and would take care of it. But the last evening of the vacation had been ruined.

By the time they returned the girl had been found. Brought home by the police. Her father had held the child close. He was the good parent. Always loved. Adil had dropped Vasundhara off and gone home.

'I'll be waiting. Come home soon,' he had said, hugging her, and Vasundhara had wondered for a moment how it would be if she just went home with Adil, if she left as she had when the girl had been younger – when she had told her husband she couldn't do it anymore. Why couldn't the little girl stay with her dad in Singapore, with his wife and new baby?

Vasundhara didn't know how to do it though, how to insist – the guilt at her failure to be a good mother had deepened over the years. It shamed her into trying and trying, despite the odds. Reluctantly, with a sinking heart, dragging her feet, she had gone inside to face a household of people who resented her.

The father and daughter were seated at the dining table. The grandmother came out of the kitchen with a tray full of food. It was the tableau of any normal family evening. Vasundhara had felt she was intruding. She didn't care about any of it. Where had the girl gone, why had she left, how had the police found her. Vasundhara had felt a bone-weary sense of disquiet and wished she could be elsewhere, not in this room with the man she had failed to love, his mother who had never liked her and the daughter who blamed her mother for all that was wrong in her little world.

'You're looking good. Love the hair. How have you been?' her ex-husband had asked, his tone kind, nice.

'Fine, really,' Vasundhara had said. The girl was touching the disfigured lump of flesh on her collarbone, the enormous dark circles making her look much older than her seven years. 'What happened here?'

'Nothing, nothing, I told Mom not to call you.'

'I went for a walk and got lost. It wasn't a big deal,' the little girl had shrugged.

'Not a big deal?' Vasundhara hadn't been able to keep her voice down. 'Your grandmother had to call the police, you were missing for ten hours and it wasn't a big deal?'

'Where's Adil? You should go home. I'll come when Daddy leaves for Singapore.' The girl might have been seven years old but the disdain in her voice was centuries old.

They had come a long, long way since then, Vasundhara and the little girl who was now a young woman. Last year when Vasundhara had to get a hysterectomy her daughter had been there for her. One night she had woken up in her hospital bed to find her sitting on the chair right beside her, her hair limp and unkempt the way it used to be when she was a little girl. Her beady eyes were boring into her mother's and Vasundhara felt the forgotten sense of dread that used to engulf her in her daughter's presence return.

'Are you okay?' she had asked, even though she was the one who had been wheeled out of surgery less than twenty-four hours back.

'I am okay,' her daughter had replied in a hoarse, unfamiliar voice. 'Or as okay as someone like me ever can be, Ma. I'm sorry.'

Her skin had been dull and pasty in the dark glow of the bedside light. She had reached out and touched the side of her mother's face, and Vasundhara had found herself recoiling. She had shut her eyes, exhausted, heavily medicated. With her daughter's clammy hand on one cheek, she had lost consciousness once again.

Vasundhara had forgotten about that night in hospital, but it came back to her today and she felt her throat dry up, wondering what her daughter was doing in the mountains with the boy she had loved so desperately but who had never quite loved her back. Not in the same way.

the woman who was unafraid of fire

Mukul thought the lockdown was a good idea. The fires, erupting on empty streets, wouldn't be able to hurt anyone. Globally, experts from various fields were working overtime to understand and resolve the problem. Mapping zones, connecting the dots, studying climate and temperature and weather patterns.

All of India was a ghost town. A stillness so extreme that my mother said she felt her apartment was buried deep at the bottom of an ocean. I was in the unchanging quiet of the hills, but it was difficult for me to fathom a silent Delhi.

'The fires are watching, the embers beneath the ground are glowing. Will the lockdown really do anything? The earth is biding its time, striking slowly – it is not in a tearing hurry,' Akshar told me, on day seven or eight of the lockdown. His statements were growing more prophetic and fanciful by the day. There was a translucence in his skin – I imagined I could see the disease in his blood moving stealthily, multiplying slowly like the fires flaring up all over the world. One more Monday had gone without a visit from Aahana. Dr Qureshi had come to check on Akshar's mother, who was running a temperature. I saw him from my window and didn't leave the room. I couldn't bear to encounter those moist marble eyes again. I felt he knew I was watching him enter the house.

I went down to meet Akshar after Dr Qureshi left. He was distraught, shaking and beside himself with grief. 'He's gone home. To Aahana. Will I ever see her again?'

The world as I knew it was in flux; I was far away from home, my mind wasn't in mint condition, so I needed to look after myself and leave this hill station as soon as I possibly could. I wasn't in the headspace to take care of Akshar. I no longer knew how to, in any case. Once upon a childhood time, when Akshar was my lifeline, it was his presence in my life that had mended me, made me teach myself to be a better person. But here we were now – sliding backwards. Not to where we used to be, to a new place of aloneness and terror.

Akshar had been reading up on the environment extensively and coming up with theories on the kind of revolution that these fires would bring about in the next couple of years. 'I am not scared of dying, Shalini. I know there are forces out there – it's all falling into place, you know. These burnings are the last in a chain that is working to put human beings in their place, to show us perspective.'

Akshar always had notions of self-grandeur, he was the most ambitious of us all in school – he already knew he was going to be famous, and I had adoringly believed back then that it would happen. Akshar with his fine mind – a philosopher, a social scientist or whatever he chose to be. He had been doing well in college too from what I gathered but then he had suddenly dropped out of the master's programme in England and came home. That phase was hazy for me. I wasn't in touch with him regularly at the time. Though now I could guess it was when he was home that first summer from university that the family secrets had exploded and his father's health collapsed. He had gone back to England after that but returned within six months and never left home again.

Akshar believed the cosmos was going to wreak a grand revenge on humankind. The sense of a prevailing malevolence on the first day here, which I had tried to push away, had returned. The mansion, its inhabitants, took on new meanings, especially at night. All of it fusing into one, the decrepit walls, the stale flesh and dry skin of those who tossed and turned in the large high-ceilinged bedrooms. I lay awake, willing myself to sleep – the footsteps were always there, tap-tap-tap, brisk, business-like.

The days were better. The sunshine of the hills. Akshar and I had been going for long walks. Staying off the roads, with the moss and grass beneath our feet. It felt safe. The tall trees, the smell of pine and sunshine. There were moments I felt as content as was possible in the circumstances. We met the *mali* in his cottage behind the mansion on one of our walks. I told him how much I admired the cosmos and Japanese lantern on the front lawn, and so many other beautiful flowers I didn't know the names for. He nodded gruffly, not very moved by my effusiveness.

'I don't think anyone here likes me very much. Ravinder, Savita, your driver, your mali,' I laughed as we made our way back for lunch.

'You've never been very likeable, Shalini,' Akshar replied.

I was wounded and lashed back childishly, sounding more stupid than hurtful. 'It's not like you are the nicest either.'

'I am charming,' Akshar shrugged.

'Fuck you're not.' I was incensed.

'I was kidding. Chill.' Akshar put an arm around my shoulders that I shrugged off.

It was becoming a pattern. Sudden acrimonious moments that ruined the mood and made us wary of each other. I knew I had grievances against Akshar, the by-product of an overwhelming, obsessive childhood love that had left indelible traces that, try as hard as I might, I couldn't let go of. It was exhausting to lie awake every night, hearing the unnerving footsteps outside my bedroom door. The dark circles under my eyes appeared deeper every morning, my hair remained thin and limp even after washing it – it was like my childhood was catching up with me in a physical, visceral manner. I disliked the mansion as if it was a living entity, one that had absorbed into its very being the discontents and hatreds and misgivings of all those who had lived within its walls over the years – all the men and women who thought the world owed them more.

Yet we had only each other. Akshar and I spent a lot of time in his study. Reading desultorily, playing Scrabble, chatting and staring out of the window – the rectangular patch of blue sky and soft green leaves looked like a painting, pastel watercolours of a still life. That window was a solace but inside the study, every moment that passed seemed to be a little less substantial, a little less real. As if we were caught in a spiral that was slowly dragging us towards some indeterminate, unreal world that existed on the fringes of life as we knew it.

Akshar's reading tastes were more eclectic than I remembered. Some old favourites he kept re-reading, but his preferred genre now was weird fiction, which I had never heard of and which I blamed for the new absurd ideas and theories he expounded to me constantly.

'The invasion of the human world by a new form of alien life is inevitable,' Akshar said to me one morning. There was also a timeless quality to our days now, one merging into another like an unorthodox movie in which one didn't quite know or care about the linearity of time. 'But we don't want to recognize the capacity these fires have – what they're telling us about our own desires, the way we have of experiencing the world, putting ourselves at the centre of it as if we aren't really the puny, insignificant creatures we were designed to be.'

I was reading Saki's short stories from a fat volume that I'd found on one of the bookshelves. My mother loved Saki but I'd never read him, perhaps precisely for that reason. The stories I chanced upon were witty, old-world. Akshar, sitting across from me, was reading Ligotti, which fed perfectly into his ideas of cosmic horror and the politics of the posthuman.

There was a temptation to humour him. To ask what these fires would teach us. To reorient ourselves and recognize that we humans didn't matter in the grand scheme of the indifferent, cold universe.

'What news of Aahana?' I asked instead to distract him, in a bid to chain him to the world we were in and not to some abstract posthuman reality.

'She will give birth soon. Which might not be a good idea under the circumstances,' Akshar said.

'Might not be a good idea under the circumstances?' My voice rose a little as I parroted his words. These abstruse statements were little proofs of the untethering of Akshar's mind – and how could I be fine if he wasn't?

'Listen to this,' Akshar continued, and started reading aloud from his book: 'These words were a revelation of the moody malignancy which until then I had no more than sensed whenever in the presence of these figures. They were singing to the "unborn in paradise", to the "pure unlived lives". They sang a dirge for existence, for all its vital forms and seasons. Their ideals were those of darkness, chaos and a melancholy half-existence consecrated to all the many shapes of death. A sea of—'

'Wait. What are you trying to say?' I found myself pinching the lump of disfigured flesh on my collarbone. I quickly took my hand away. It was a childhood habit I had outgrown, of worrying the wound till it bled whenever I was disturbed. The words were heavy, they filled me with gloom yet I didn't understand them, and I had no idea why Akshar was reading them out with such a strong sense of purpose.

He looked disappointed. I felt like a prized student who had suddenly let her teacher down. 'I am reading from Ligotti's *The Last Feast of Harlequin*. He wrote it in 1990 but when I read those lines, I feel he's talking to us, in this moment, when the world has been brought to a standstill by fire. And I sense a special message for me and Aahana. Telling us to let the unborn remain in paradise, not bring it to this burning disease-ridden earth, to death.'

I understood what he was saying, even though I didn't want to. Understanding him made me complicit in his worldview, his conspiracy theories. I wanted out, to get away from Akshar, his mansion. His batshit talk was crushing something inside me, making me remember things I didn't want to – snapshots from my childhood that I had labelled DANGEROUS and put away and promised I would never revisit, never allow to have power over me again.

And that was the mood in which I went up to bed, up the stairs and down the dark, dank corridor. Every night, I would speak to Mukul, who would get worried about how garbled and confused I sounded. I resolved to speak to him in the mornings only, when my room was bathed in sunlight. Not at night when I was all on edge. And then a measure of relief as the footsteps came. Relief just because I felt in that moment that I couldn't have waited for one second more. Slowly, the steps drew closer and closer – there was the smallest of pauses outside my door, a slight break in the rhythm, and I burrowed into my quilt and covered my ears until the sound receded, till they returned down the corridor. Another little pause, and then it was gone.

Those footsteps needed to stop. I had to figure out how to stop them.

Aahana arrived the next day. She was no longer the glowing, beautiful, animated woman I remembered from a few weeks ago. The change was so stark that I wondered if my mind, insomniac and nervous, was playing games with me. Aahana's face was pinched and white, her hair uncombed, her stomach enormous, with two skinny arms on either side, propped up by matchstick legs. She seemed to have shrunk while her stomach had grown huge, as if there was a monster inside it, sucking the life out of her.

Akshar didn't seem to notice or become alarmed. His eyes softened with love as they rested on his beloved's face. I felt a sharp pang somewhere within.

Aahana kept looking over her shoulder as if some wild animal was on her trail. She largely ignored my presence, which I didn't find offensive – she was hardly there herself. I expected Akshar to pull himself together and comfort her – not rant the way he had been doing the last few days – but that didn't happen.

'Aahana, I was wondering if Reyhan might be over-medicating me with the intention of hastening my demise?' he casually asked Aahana once we had settled down in the back lawn with chai and pakoras. I wanted to escape to my room. Maybe in fifteen minutes or so I could pretend to suddenly remember some work I had to do.

'Oh please, Akshar,' Aahana said, sounding resigned. 'How do you expect me to go home after you've put that idea into my head?'

'Stay with me. Don't go home.'

'You don't mean that, do you?' Aahana's voice was soft and wistful, and for the first time since I had met her, I felt a sliver of sympathy. It couldn't be easy, her life. I resented her, I couldn't quite view her without envy, yet I knew it had to be hard – in love with her half-brother for years, suddenly pregnant and married to someone else out of desperation. And now the only person she really cared for was dying on her. The moment of understanding soon passed, though. They had made their choice; with this love that was cloying and undying. Nothing is destiny, we all make the beds we lie on.

'I think I do mean it,' Akshar said. 'Things are changing – end times are near. Nothing quite matters anymore.'

If I had expected Aahana to rubbish what Akshar had just said it didn't happen. She replied, 'I know, these fires, we are all going to lose our sanity, whether we burn to death or not.'

Akshar shook his head. His theory was more empirical than that. I guessed we were in for another round of psychotic mansplaining and I wasn't wrong.

'It is going to make us all go mad but none of this is random,' he embarked. 'We don't need Netflix to tell us horror stories, the world has always been horrific and these fires, every little flame, is here with a purpose. They've burst forth into the world as we know it, forcing people to change their ways – be alone, isolate, reflect on the foolishness that is human life. The fires will spread, slowly, insidiously; people will cough, burn and struggle to breathe, they will change, they will know there is no way out of the meaninglessness of it all. And as people slowly mutate, forced to confront the real horrors of existence, they will, inevitably, become grotesque versions of their former selves, and they will succumb – to the fire or to the madness within, which they can no longer control.'

The intense glittering of Akshar's eyes was mirrored in Aahana's as she hung on to his every word. I had hoped Aahana might laugh her charming laugh, lay a calming hand on his arm and ask him to chill. But there was no question of that. If he was the leader of this doomsday cult, she was his most willing disciple. And if I was honest, so was I, but a struggling disciple who knew better than them what fires could do, how they could destroy families, lives. I knew the power of a single matchstick.

'Baby-ji, juice *peeyoge*?' Ravinder materialized from somewhere in that quiet manner he did and was looking lovingly at Aahana.

'*Nahi*, thank you, Ravinder,' Aahana pouted at the elderly man. She started asking him questions about his family and in the next few minutes I had the answers to all the questions I had received monosyllabic replies to, from Savita and him. Savita had digestive troubles that never seemed to get better. I wanted to ask if the dubious Reyhan treated her too and sniggered to myself. Ravinder was worried about his two older sons and their wives, who were daily-wage labourers in Delhi and out of jobs now, thanks to the lockdown.

'Akshar, why aren't you asking them to come home?' Aahana asked when Ravinder had left. 'His sons and their families?'

'Of course I've asked,' Akshar said, frowning. 'But they have wives and small babies. How will they come? The roads are unsafe and there are restrictions.'

I got up saying I had to send off some creatives to the office. I needed to be alone. The conversation segueing to the minutiae of the everyday was as uncomfortable as the highbrow exposition of the meaninglessness of life – Akshar and Aahana, an ideal partnership like no other, connected on every level, now conversing like a married couple at the breakfast table on the travails of the house help. I didn't mean to be a bitch but it was quite intolerable, all of it.

When I reached my floor, I saw that the nurse was about to enter Akshar's mother's room. She nodded at me. I could have nodded back and carried on, but I found myself going towards her.

'How's she?' I asked, pointing my chin at the door and beyond. I imagined Akshar's mother walking around inside, touching and picking things up from the side tables, restless, at a loss.

'Come and meet her?' the nurse suggested. She had a kind face, which was comforting.

Akshar's mother was lying down, not sitting ramrod straight on the bed like the other day. Her eyes were wide open and she was staring at the ceiling, her lips moving, though she wasn't speaking out loud.

'See who's here to meet you,' the nurse said.

Akshar's mother sat up in one fluid movement. She looked at me and smiled.

'We did have fun in London, didn't we?' she said. Her voice had the remnants of a British accent that had faded over the years. I hadn't noticed it the last time.

'Yes,' I smiled. 'We did.'

'I don't want to go back to Avyukt, don't send me back,' she whispered.

'But don't you want to see Akshar, your son?' I asked, knowing very well what their relationship had been like – I needn't have. I couldn't get myself to mention Sahil at all even though I know he was her favourite.

'He was a beautiful baby,' she said, her features softening with maternal love that was unexpected. And then just as suddenly she became enraged, got off the bed and looked to her right and left, as if searching for something. 'But they took him away. Avyukt and that girl – they hated me and I hated them. My mother told me not to leave London. But did I listen to her? No. But now I'm staying with her. With my mother. That is a good thing.'

Motherhood wasn't something I understood. The idea of a grey-haired woman, away from her parents for decades, yet in her most vulnerable moments of senility, craving her mother.

'Does no one come to meet her?' I asked the nurse.

'Some neighbours do – that girl's mother, she comes. Once in a while. Maybe once in two or three months,' the nurse replied. 'No relatives, not even one.'

'Which girl?'

'The … that Aahana? Her mother.' The nurse looked at me, unsure if she had said too much. Meher. Aahana's mother. I had assumed there would be no love lost between the two women. But with age is supposed to come grace and wisdom – who knows what made Meher visit her old friend, her erstwhile lover's wife?

'Isn't this lonely for you too?' I asked the nurse.

'My son lives in town. I visit him on weekends, when the agency sends a replacement nurse for one night. That's good enough for me,' the nurse replied. 'But Aunty can be difficult. Some days the way she curses – by god, I start blushing. And the things she says – about her husband, her son. You mustn't tell her son I told you this but she does have a wicked tongue.'

She was speaking in a Hindi that I wasn't quite used to – a hill dialect. Akshar's mother was listening to us chat. I wasn't sure how much she understood but she knew she was being spoken about.

'This is wrong,' she said rather imperiously. 'I won't tolerate it. You can leave right now.'

'I can leave right now, then who will give you your medicines and food and bathe you?' asked the nurse in a jocular, patient-bedside voice.

'She will,' replied Akshar's mother, looking at me. I smiled at her. She moved me in ways I couldn't explain. Her heavy past – of loss, of neglect – and this present in which she had risen above it all with insanity and the powerful tool of forgetting. 'Won't you?'

'Of course I will,' I said.

'Everyone hates me. I want to burn the house down,' she said in a pleasant voice. I felt a chill go down my spine. Her comments, sometimes crazy, sometimes lucid, disconnected and senseless, brought back visions and memories that I didn't want.

'I sometimes hear you walking up and down the corridor at night,' I said to the nurse in a bid to clear my mind.

'Oh I'm sorry, I hope it doesn't disturb you?' I felt a flood of relief. I hadn't realized that I was desperate to confirm who the night walker was, that the footsteps were not some apparition or a figment of my impending insanity.

'Not at all,' I smiled, trying not to appear too delighted.

'Tonight you will be spared,' she said, sounding happy too. 'I'll be leaving as soon as the other nurse arrives.'

'Oh, is it Saturday then?' I was losing track of the days – it was impossible to differentiate between workdays and weekends anymore. I did get calls from office asking for files and creatives, meetings were set up on Zoom which I attended – everyone sitting in tiny rectangular boxes, like private cells in a prison block. Mukul said he and his team were working pretty much as usual; productivity wasn't down.

'It is Saturday,' the nurse confirmed.

'But how will you get home?' I asked. The lockdown was severe – no public or private transport was plying the roads.

'It's just a four kilometre walk,' she replied. 'I will leave soon, in an hour, so I can reach home before it gets dark.'

'You aren't worried about the fires?'

The nurse shrugged. 'Whatever will be, will be.'

Akshar's mother was lying down on the bed now, her face towards the wall.

'I should go,' I said, getting up. 'Have a good weekend. I'll drop by again for a chat on Monday, perhaps.'

'Yes, yes, that will be good,' she replied. 'I'll be back tomorrow evening. See you.'

I returned to my room slowly. I didn't know when Aahana would leave. I wanted to go down only after she did. On a rare impulse I phoned my mother, who was so happy I'd called. Seeing Akshar's mother had filled me with strange regrets, her rambling and strange words that had no place in a rational world.

I went downstairs at 7:30 p.m. Akshar was alone in his study, a glass of wine in his hand and a half-finished bottle beside him. 'Shalini,' he said. 'I decided not to badger you. To let you join me when you felt like it.'

'And here I am.'

'Aahana left. We had a disagreement.'

'Oh,' I said wearily and added the obligatory 'But why?'

'She wants to have this baby. I was telling her she shouldn't.'

'How can she not?' I asked. 'She looks like she is going to deliver any day. How can she not have the baby?'

'There are ways,' said Akshar, shaking his head grimly. 'Humanity is losing – it can't win against fire, one of the most elemental forces of nature, can it? Ultimately, technology and the medical sciences will have to acknowledge defeat. So let us not disturb the order of the natural world any more than we already have – let things stay as they are, let nothing new infect the earth. Birth now can only be hideous, an aberration.'

'Akshar, I signed the document the other day – I'm a trustee of your will, I'll make sure your baby gets his or her due.' I was desperate to bring Akshar back to the world as he had seen it, just a few weeks back. There was a flicker in his eyes.

'Yes, Shalini, if things go back to the way they were, then you will be there for my child, I know that,' he said, as if placating me. 'But you do see it's not possible anymore. These burnings? They are the finale, an inhuman elemental revolution that will end it all. The world has reached its zenith of greed, of capitalism and plundering. So let it be. I, in any case, have nothing to lose. I am already nearing the end.'

By the time I went upstairs after dinner it was 11 p.m. It was a particularly cold night. Lying with my quilt up to my nose I could see the night sky, the full moon and the glittering stars. This was my nightly ritual – staring at the sky till I felt drowsy and soothed, and my eyes got heavy with sleep. I shut my eyes and what I saw was fire; vicious, hot, the flames hard and distinct, and then blurring, melting into the darkness. After that, I heard (or thought I did) soft footsteps approaching my door. I knew I was mistaken; the nurse had said she was going to be away tonight. But as I snuggled down, the footsteps didn't go away. They got louder the way they would if a person was coming nearer.

The footsteps stopped at my door. This had never happened. They were supposed to continue past my door. My throat dried up. I propped myself up on my elbows and looked at the door, at the thin horizontal line of yellow light at the bottom – like a flaming column, like the fire was already at my door. My eyes were used to the darkness and in the dark moonlight that flooded the room, I could see – or perhaps sense more than see – the door handle being pushed down. I always locked the door when I came into the room. The handle rattled a little but even if someone was pushing the door, it was locked and wouldn't open. There was a soft knock. I pictured the door creaking open.

I felt a relentless sweaty fear, deep, bottomless. The door was still shut and the knock came again, more insistent this time but still so soft that it left room for me to think I'd imagined it. I heard a deep, mournful sigh and then the footsteps again, this time receding. The air inside the room seemed to thicken. Heavy with moisture and the faint smell of smoke. I heard a tinkling laugh and realized it was I who had laughed out loud, one of those pointless polite laughs that one performs at a party while sipping wine. I pulled the quilt over my head, shut my eyes and lay awake for what felt like hours, till the night sky started fading, changing colour, preparing for dawn. I finally fell asleep; a dark, lugubrious, fitful sleep, from which I would wake in a few hours, unrefreshed.

7

the woman in the room

The woman was craving a drink. The days when she was most lucid were the worst in some ways. She wanted a single malt, large, with one cube of ice. In the winter she didn't need the ice. She knew the time of year from the air, the taste of it. Today she could tell Akshar was in the house, she could sense his presence the way she could the season. Not like some other days when she didn't know if he was alive or dead or even if she had ever had a son other than Sahil. He was probably in his father's study. Moralistic little prick. He had frowned on his mother's drinking. Called her an alcoholic. As if his dad, his hero, wasn't one too.

She wished she was in the large terrace in front of her old room, which had the most gorgeous view of the cold, ragged mountains. With an easel in front of her and a drink in her hand. She had long taught herself not to need people. She had not even succeeded in loving and caring for her son, in embracing the easiest thing which most women not just managed but revelled in, felt empowered by – motherhood. It was only after Sahil was born that she had realized what that meant. The weighty, socially sanctioned events in her life had not given her the happiness that the incidental, accidental ones had.

As a newlywed she had fallen in love with the mountains, though. It was the only tribute to her husband that she could boast of. He had passed on his love for the hills to his wife and that love, in turn, had long outlived her love for him. On her lucid days she took in a lungful of mountain air and had no complaints. Except that the room with a view was no longer hers. She had been told it was Akshar's bedroom now.

'Aahana stays with him?' she asked the nurse conversationally one day when she remembered more than usual.

'No, she married Dr Qureshi,' said the nurse.

'It was impossible for me to like Aahana. How could I, a woman who barely managed to love her son, like his girlfriend, his half-sister, my husband's daughter?'

The nurse shook her head, her mouth a straight line of disapproval.

The woman sat back, tired. That was enough. Of thoughts and sharing. She felt the familiar shadows descending and welcomed them. It was so much nicer to just forget.

the woman who left

Vasundhara was not able to sleep till she popped a pill at night. But then the nightmares started again. New ones, inspired by the fires that were raging around the world. It felt like the fire that had led to her biggest personal loss – that had lay dormant all this time – was now consuming the whole world, as if it had triggered something that the world couldn't control anymore. It was fanciful thinking; she knew it was rubbish. In one dream, her daughter stood in the middle of a fire, surrounded by flames, calling out to her, asking her to come, but Vasundhara, drugged and asleep, was not able to move a limb. In another Vasundhara's eyelids were stitched up with white thread and as she tried to get to her daughter who was screaming for her, the doors and windows of the room she was in became stone walls. She was left to claw her way along, hoping to find the door that was no longer there.

The next night, Vasundhara didn't take a pill. Besides, she was worried that her daughter might phone and she, knocked out by the medication, would fail to take the call. She sat at her desk, scrolling through Facebook aimlessly, looking at people's posts on fires they had witnessed or memorial posts for family they had lost to a fire. She read articles on Twitter. One warned of an impending water crisis and how that would affect rescue operations and the work of hospitals. 'It's normal to feel anxious in these times; if you didn't that would be more worrying', she read in another. Right, good to know. Many told her that what would help would be to have a routine. Who didn't know that, Vasundhara shook her head impatiently.

With every passing year the frequent, frenzied eruptions that Shalini had been prone to had reduced. Her personality had solidified into one that was socially acceptable, even pleasant. The last time Vasundhara had had to rush to her side was ten years back, when Shalini had almost been asphyxiated to death by a fire that had broken out in her hostel wing at college. She couldn't remember any other crisis after that – none from which her daughter had to painstakingly rethink and restart her life once more. Shalini had landed a great internship in her final year of design school, got a job that paid well, dated some nice guys – though when the relationships didn't last she wasn't plunged into despair. The acrimonious, angry relationship between mother and daughter had slowly settled into one that was quieter, even laced with understanding. Yet how could Vasundhara not know how brittle Shalini's mind was, how easily it shattered, despite all the progress she had made. She knew the fires didn't bode well for the world at large but for her daughter, they could spell doom like for no one else. It was past 11 p.m. On an impulse she called Shalini's number. She suddenly, desperately, needed to know she was fine.

The phone kept ringing. After all it was late. She was about to disconnect when Shalini answered. 'Ma?' she asked, accompanied by the sound of heavy breathing. Shalini was taking deep, laboured breaths.

'Shalini, what happened? Tell me ...'

That was when Vasundhara knew it was beginning again. Shalini's voice was hoarse, loud. 'No, no, no, Ma, no. Stop. No, no, no, no. No more please.'

Vasundhara's blood ran cold, her head feeling like it was going to burst. 'What? Shalini, what?' Her daughter was quiet now. She didn't reply.

But then she screamed, a long, shrill scream – loud, so very high-pitched. Vasundhara stood up. That scream, it took her back. To the little girl who would just scream and scream and no one knew why. After what felt like ages, Shalini stopped screaming. There was silence. Then the line disconnected.

Vasundhara's mind had folded up. She couldn't breathe, couldn't think, nothing. She didn't know how long she sat like that – immobile and comatose. Her phone rang. Her hands were shaking as she took the call. It was Shalini. She now spoke in a normal voice, 'Sorry, Ma, don't worry. I don't know what came over me. Okay?'

'Shalini …' Vasundhara whispered.

'I am so sorry,' Shalini sounded really contrite. Cheerful almost. 'I'm going to sleep now. Speak to you later.'

Vasundhara knew the moment the call ended that she had to go to the hills, to Shalini. Tomorrow morning, she would see how to make arrangements in the middle of the lockdown but there had to be a way. Her daughter was at this very moment a ticking bomb. Vasundhara's exhausted mind told her she had to get to her before it was too late.

the woman who was unafraid of fire

I woke up to the sound of my phone ringing. With my eyes still half-shut, I groped around for it among the sheets and swiped to accept the call.

'Are you still asleep?' asked Mukul, as if I was enjoying a languorous beauty sleep or something.

'I barely slept,' I mumbled. I opened my eyes and looked at the bedroom door. I remembered the footsteps, the handle moving downwards, the gust of a sigh.

'What happened? Your mother called, she's so worried about you,' he said. I felt a twinge of remorse. I didn't want to remember how I'd behaved when my mother had called last night.

'Why? What did she say?' My muscles clenched. I hoped she hadn't said too much.

'Nothing really. Just ... she seems worried about you. How you're doing. Asked if I speak to you often. Whether you sound fine to me,' Mukul said. I felt a sense of relief. I wouldn't have forgiven her if she'd said anything more than that. But then, she wouldn't. She was too ashamed of me for that.

I spoke to Mukul from force of habit but with each passing day I felt a little more disconnected, more aware that our realities were very different now. Mukul would have no idea how hard it was for someone like me to live in this place of doom. My mother, she knew.

I was fearful, tired and decrepit – so many adjectives to describe one single mind and none of them uplifting. I looked out of the window. The crisp mountain sun appeared sickly today, as if the smoke from the fires was polluting it too.

When I went downstairs Akshar was pacing up and down the corridor outside the dining room. 'Today's the due date,' he said upon seeing me, as if carrying on a conversation we'd been having.

'Aahana's? The baby's?' I asked tiredly. Which was the correct usage anyway – was the mother due for the cutting up of her body, for separation from the baby? Or the baby due for entry into our fire-ridden world?

'But there's no need for it,' Akshar said firmly. 'Aahana told me the baby is no longer moving.'

I didn't have the bandwidth to deal with this, not that I cared about Aahana or her baby. 'Is she in the hospital?' I asked.

'Waste of time, hospitals,' he muttered. 'She *is* going, though, to the hospital – says she's feeling awful, can't do this anymore. Everything seems wrong, is what she said. Which, of course, is correct and inevitable. She was weeping and incoherent, but what can be done? The earth will have its way, the fire will have its way.'

'Let's go for a walk, Akshar,' I said. I wanted to get out. Away from this diseased mansion. To sunshine, to the clean air outside.

Soon, we stood in the driveway deciding which way to go. 'Do you want to head out from the main gate? We don't have to walk within the property every time.'

'Is that not … risky?' I didn't think I could deal with another fire.

'It's a risk we must learn to take,' Akshar said. 'We can't just hide away forever.'

We set out, following the long-winded path down to the main gate. When we were on the other side of the imposing gate and the guard had stopped saluting Akshar, I looked back at the mansion. Far away and partially obscured by tall trees, the mansion looked like an enchanted gingerbread house, buried deep in the woods. Distant and toothless, not the malignant being that I knew it to be.

Akshar seemed to cheer up once we were outside, as if some essential lifeblood had returned to him, in getting away from his desolate home. We spoke of the wild – it had drawn us close as teenagers, our love for wolves and crocodiles, for forests and waves breaking on unnamed shores. The unthinking, pure cruelty of the natural world fascinated us as we leaned against the craggy precipices outsides our school boundary wall and talked our heads off. I was ridiculously happy to realize those memories had stayed with Akshar as well. We spoke of school, too, of course, of Jugaad as always, our beautiful friend and child through our school days.

'Remember the day Jugaad died?' Akshar asked. I didn't want to. We were talking of so much that used to be close to our hearts today, laughing a little as we walked down narrow mountain roads that led towards valleys and hamlets where people led normal lives. Though I didn't quite know what normal really meant.

'I don't want to. I don't want to remember that last day. He led a happy, full life and that's enough for me.'

'Yes, exactly,' said Akshar eagerly. 'And we buried him in the backyard, what remained of him, behind the school – where he had always belonged. He was like our son, Shalini. I want to do the same for my other child, I don't want Reyhan to bury him, I want to bring him to my home, to bury him in the garden of the house where his forefathers lived.'

I felt myself deflate, like one of those air-filled dolls when their round plastic knob is pulled out and all the air leaves slowly, with a low whistle. All the fresh mountain air seemed to disappear from around me too, and I was left in a vacuum from which I struggled to speak.

'Akshar, what are you even saying? Aahana, she came to see you yesterday – she is pregnant, full term. How can you talk of burial? The baby …' It amazed me, this morbid assumption of the death of his own baby which was, likely, still safe in its mother's womb.

'I told you, Shalini. Aahana must be in the hospital by now. I felt she shouldn't go but it's okay. It's her decision. It's not easy to understand, what is happening, it's too insidious … anyway no one will be spared so doesn't really matter – crouch at home or be out and about, it will find you eventually.'

'But what is going to happen … you know, with these fires?' I didn't know what I was asking or why. In any case Akshar had been answering this question for weeks now and he was more than happy to take off again.

'I'm closing in on death and with that comes a certain kind of enlightenment. My death and the supposed birth of my child, I have come to realize, are linked – that does give me a sort of special, grotesque vision.' He seemed to hesitate for a moment but then he spoke again. 'I have been trying not to say this but Shalini, you know you are one of the special ones too. You've had a connection with fire since childhood.'

I had been expecting this. I had known Akshar would dig this up one day. I said, 'I don't want to think about that. It's the one thing I don't want to think about, you know that.'

Akshar smiled and patted my head as if I was a child. 'Yes, yes, you don't have to think about it. Not if you don't want to. I just meant to say that my desire for knowledge of the world beyond the human – because I am at the threshold – has made me more receptive to the burnings and the way the world will eventually lose itself in them.'

'I … I think … how can you be so sure, Akshar? It's all conjecture, all these theories you have, no?' I was desperate to not believe but somewhere inside I felt what Akshar was saying made perfect sense. Perhaps because I was one of the chosen ones, as he had claimed.

'I sense what the fires are doing, Shalini, they're moving slowly now … claiming lives but it's not enough, they need *more*, every day they need more. They are hungry. They're on a mission. But first they have to isolate; separate friends, lovers, families. Alone, vulnerable, exposed to evil, we will succumb. The lonely, the cautious, the fearful – they will suffer the most, they will know what is happening and be helpless in the face of it. But eventually no one is going to escape the wrath of the fires. Nothing very prolonged, maybe a couple of years it will take, four or five at most.'

I was listening to Akshar so attentively, slavishly, that I didn't see the car coming around the bend. Akshar pulled me to one side as it came to a theatrical screeching halt and Dr Qureshi got out. He glanced in my direction but spoke only to Akshar. 'Why are you taking unnecessary risks, walking around like this? Anyway, I am going to see Aahana. In the hospital. Would you like to come?'

I wondered in what capacity Dr Qureshi was asking – as his wife's half-brother or her lover or best friend or as the father of her baby? The possibilities were infinite. It depended on what Reyhan Qureshi knew and what he didn't. Those glossy marble eyes missed little. I wouldn't be surprised if he knew it all.

Akshar narrowed his eyes and shook his head as if he had been asked a trick question he refused to fall for. Reyhan Qureshi frowned, his eyebrows furrowing together, but one corner of his mouth lifted in a smirk that seemed to say: and this is how much you love her.

'How is Aahana doing?' I asked, hoping to break the hostile silence between the two men.

Dr Qureshi turned his cold eyes on me but answered politely. 'Not very well. The baby ... well, the gynecologist is trying to assess the situation. Things aren't looking very good.'

Akshar turned to me a little triumphantly, as if to say 'I told you so'. It was hard to believe in that moment that Aahana was the one in the nursing home – the Aahana whom Akshar loved to distraction and forever. And especially knowing that the baby was his, for whom he had gone out of his way to drag me here, to set up a trust, to make sure the child would be cared for after he was long gone. It was as if the burnings were wiping away all that mattered to Akshar – they had had their way with him already, pushing his entire being into a dark corner where love, affection and all the light within him had been replaced with a vile, selfish enlightenment.

'I'm sorry,' I said to the doctor. 'Give her my best, please. And oh, I'm Shalini. We've not been introduced …'

'I know. Reyhan.' He held his hand out and I shook it, more as a marker of formally recognizing each other's existence. Akshar looked impatient, as if he couldn't wait for Reyhan to leave.

'I told her there's no point in going to the hospital,' Akshar said, not for the first time, as Reyhan got into his car and shut the door. 'If anything, these fires might get to her sooner – they're lurking outside hospitals to capture the weak, those who are already debilitated.'

I had read a report online on how the roads in front of hospitals and police stations were particularly compromised, the places that couldn't be avoid in emergencies. The report had freaked people out; they were demanding proof, and rightly so.

'You won't even go meet her?'

'There's no point in hastening my death as well. Let me be here for a few more days – if Aahana returns from the hospital, she will need me by her side.'

'She hasn't lost the baby,' I insisted. 'Dr Qureshi just said she's not doing well, not like it's critical.'

Akshar gave me a pitying look, as if it were my lover and child whose lives were in jeopardy. 'Let's go home, Shalini.'

As we made our way back, we came across a group of women sitting in a circle around a pile of ashes and embers at a hairpin bend where the road had widened and was jutting out. They were wearing earth colours and bright neckpieces and bracelets that jangled and clinked rhythmically as they raised their hands skywards. Sonorous, deep and beautiful chanting filled the cold mournful mountain air – though I couldn't follow what they were saying, it suffused my very being with light and strength. A sense of peace that I had possibly never felt in my life before.

Akshar nodded at them but they didn't acknowledge us. 'There was a fire here last night. No lives were lost. They are appeasing the earth now.'

'How do you know?'

'I can follow what they're saying, no?' Akshar replied.

The view from that corner was spectacular too. The valley below, the mountain ranges across from us, the sun, the mist, the little cottages that clung to the mountainside like 3D fridge magnets.

The sense of beauty and peace that I was feeling dissipated into the cold air as we approached the mansion. We climbed the road to the stately driveway, leaving behind the tall trees and their shadows to come face-to-face with those windows that looked like misshapen, unblinking eyes. I felt a deep foreboding like when I'd arrived here – what was it, fifteen or twenty days back? Only this time it was more defined, the aversion I felt as I looked upon the house. An uneasy fear and loathing of what I knew lay inside – the dank corridors, the swollen walls, the relentless footsteps, the demented woman pacing in her dimly lit room, the hostile presence of Ravinder and Savita. I wanted to stay out, delay going inside for as long as possible, but it was well past lunchtime and Ravinder would be waiting – quiet, disapproving, as was his permanent mien in my presence – but waiting patiently nevertheless, to re-heat the food for his beloved master, and by grudging default, for me as well.

We were sitting in the living room after dinner. In brighter ages this room might have hosted many parties but now it was a sorrowful place with large, dusty chandeliers and way too many sofas, all plump, overstuffed yet sagging. Akshar had dug up a bunch of old records and we were listening to music on his dad's turntable – those LP players on which one has to carefully drop the needle at the right place, or it makes a scratching sound till the pin shifts and settles as it should. I was not into classical music but the notes of Beethoven's fifth symphony were comfortingly familiar.

Akshar was leaning back in a soft leather armchair with his eyes shut. The deep frown lines between his eyebrows were gone for the moment; his profile, in repose, was beautiful. His mind was in a strange unknown place, and faithful as ever, I was slowly but surely following him to the broken realms to which it was wandering.

I had picked up an old *Reader's Digest* that was lying around. I was half-reading it when Akshar suddenly opened his eyes, leaned forward and said, 'We lost the baby.'

I felt that curious dropping sensation in the stomach that one gets on rollercoaster rides. I didn't say anything, just waited for Akshar to carry on.

'I got a call from the hospital right before you came down for dinner,' he continued, almost cheerfully. 'It was Reyhan. He sounded distraught. Was going on and on. Quite incoherent. I asked if the baby could be buried in our garden. He stuttered something or the other and when I asked him once again, then hung up.'

'You've known this for the last hour?' I couldn't believe we'd been eating and talking as per usual, while the news of the baby's death was nestled in Akshar's head. He hadn't thought it necessary to tell me at all, not till an hour had passed, when he'd decided to mention it as casually as gossip about a distant relative.

'Yes. Well, it was a matter of time. Apparently, it was hard on Aahana, having to push out a dead baby,' Akshar said. Anything being hard on Aahana would have made Akshar wring his hands and rave and rant, even two weeks back. But he was a man obsessed with apocalyptic thoughts of burnings now. He couldn't quite focus on the specificities of human experiences anymore.

'You still won't go to the hospital?'

'I don't think there's any point now. Aahana will be drugged. There will be paperwork but that's for Reyhan to complete. I can't get the baby home till tomorrow I think.'

'Akshar, has Reyhan known all along that the baby is yours?'

'No, but I'll tell him tomorrow morning if he fusses about it being buried here.'

I don't know how long we might have gone on, back and forth, not making sense to each other but speaking because we were too scared – or at least I was – to be silent. But there were raised voices in the foyer outside, then the sound of quick footsteps. The heavy oak door to the living room pushed open and Reyhan entered, followed by Ravinder who looked nervous and confused.

'It's okay, Ravinder, I am sure Dr Qureshi has a good reason for this late-night visit.' Akshar spoke in their brand of hilly Hindi and Ravinder, visibly relieved, nodded and retreated.

Reyhan Qureshi's moist eyes were bulging in a way that was amphibian and unpleasant. The splendid chandeliers, lifeless and dull, were never switched on in this erstwhile grand room and in the dim lighting of a few lamps mounted on the walls, it looked like the lower half of his face had melted away, leaving only those awful eyes, which were glistening with naked hatred towards Akshar.

'You are going to pay for this. For what you've done. Both you and my wife.' He spat out the words 'my wife' and turned to leave the room. It seemed that was all he had wanted to say. At the end of a long, exhausting day, he had come to Akshar's mansion just to promise revenge in a few pithy words. As he reached the door, he tripped on the faded brown doormat and spun around so he was looking at Akshar once more. 'You can go to the hospital in the morning and collect your dead son. Do whatever you want with the body. It's of no use to me.'

'Aahana told you?' Akshar lifted one eyebrow. It was like a scene from a badly made horror movie: the cold decadence of this mansion and then Reyhan tripping on the mat – the comic tragedy of it all.

'She did,' Reyhan said and left the room. The door banged shut behind him. He must have pushed it, an oddly childish thing to do. I had a sudden memory of my mother shouting at me for banging my bedroom door, trying to force me to come out of my room. As if she could. A common childhood memory for many sullen, brattish kids. Though my childhood was different; it wasn't that I was a brat, it was much more than that.

Akshar looked at me and said, 'That's done then. Good.'

I needn't have come here at all; there was going to be no trust fund, no need for trustees. The elaborate signing of the trust deed in the garden with the affable Rana, slightly tipsy on beer, felt like a charade that could have been avoided. I tiredly rubbed my eyes and was about to speak when I realized Akshar was talking in a low monotone.

I half-listened to Akshar's words, words that I'd grown used to in the last week. The sentences were long and convoluted and hard to follow but the words were not – burnings, death, horror, cosmos, design, childbirth, evil, implosion. Long improvised dirges that would ring in my ears forever. As he spoke, Akshar's voice grew louder, wilder, like a symphony that rises and subsides. Sometimes he would seem to gasp for air, breathless; pause for minutes altogether so I thought he was done till he started again.

When he was finally too exhausted to speak anymore, I got up to leave. 'Won't you go to bed now, Akshar?'

'I don't know if I can,' he replied. 'You have a good night's sleep, Shalini, and tomorrow morning we'll have the burial when I return from the hospital.'

'Where?' I asked, my heart sinking for the hundredth time.

'Oh, I selected a patch behind the mansion. I've already asked the gardener to dig the ground and keep it ready.'

'You did this before you knew the baby was dead?'

Akshar sighed; he was so done with my questions.

'And no religious ceremony …' I petered off. I practised no religion but I did know there were rituals associated with death. Akshar laughed, not a pleasant laugh.

'No, just a burial,' he said. 'Don't worry I don't belong to any cult. No chanting, no ritualistic jumping around. Just a burial.'

Well, that would be okay – there was no need for ritual for someone who had never lived. I leaned down and gave Akshar a hug. His arms came around me and we held each other tight. I inhaled the familiar clean Akshar smell. When I straightened up, Akshar was sitting straight in the chair, eyes blank except for a feverish light.

I took a few steps towards the door but was loath to leave Akshar alone. I stood in the middle of the room, uncertain. My mind was like a sieve, I couldn't hold on to a single thought, one came and was replaced by another as quickly. From Aahana to the gardener to a cold hospital room to Akshar's mother.

'"The mind is restless, Krishna",' I muttered. I'd read that in Upamanyu Chatterjee's *English August* when I was a teenager and the line, it got stuck in my mind forever. I knew it was from the Bhagavad Gita but for me, it epitomized and seamlessly meshed my teen angst and that of Agastya Sen in Madna, the hottest town in the country.

'What are you thinking, Shalini?' Akshar asked with a half-smile.

'Of Agastya Sen?' It made no sense without context and barely any with, but he nodded. 'How much we loved that book, Akshar.'

'I'll go to bed after all,' he said, getting up. 'Tomorrow will be a long day.'

When we reached the first-floor landing, he leaned in to give me another tight hug before we parted. This time, as we loosened our hold on each other, I reached up to give him a quick kiss which landed on the side of his mouth. Akshar cupped my face, bent down and kissed me. It was like a first kiss, tentative, exploratory, but it was like coming home after a long hard day's work, restorative. Akshar deepened the kiss as we held on to each other, not quite able to let go. It was a long, long kiss; lingering, hungry, yet it was only that. When we let go of each other what remained was a lot of love and a bit of longing, at least for me. A taste of Akshar in my mouth. For Akshar it may have spelt only comfort. I'll never know.

'I will always love you, Akshar,' I said, and he lightly touched the heart-shaped little lump of disfigured flesh on my collarbone as he used to in school. I had never allowed anyone apart from Akshar to touch it.

I wanted to be grown up about this but what was returning, suddenly, was the dark feeling of abandonment and loss that had been my constant companion since I was born. My love for Akshar – intense, deep – and his unquestioning acceptance of it, like a god accepting worship, had worked well at a time when I'd desperately needed something to believe in. Akshar had allowed me, in his trademark selfish way, to get over myself. Our lopsided yet marvellous relationship had made me a better person in untold ways, for which I was grateful. My mother, who had instinctively disliked Akshar, had also recognized this – that it was my love for Akshar which had made me more human, a better person, as far as was possible for a child born so strange.

But I didn't want those pre-Akshar feelings to return – the desperation, the haunting sense of being unlovable, of abandonment by all those who should have been there for me. Memories of a mother who had loved her boyfriend more than she did her own child. And fire. Then and now.

8

the woman in the room

It was only 8 a.m. but the nurse was already tired. One of those days.

'Thank you, Amma,' said the woman as the nurse served her breakfast. 'The baby kept me up all night. I didn't have the energy to go downstairs to the dining room.'

She called her own mother Mummy and spoke to her much more often. But the days when Amma entered the room never went well.

'Why do you hate me so much?' she said balefully after a while, looking straight at the nurse. She picked up a pillow and held it out. 'Take him, keep him. I don't care. If you don't like the way I'm doing this, do it yourself.'

The nurse took the pillow. When episodes like this had first occurred, she had tried to correct the woman, tell her what was what, that she was imagining things. Now she knew it was easiest to play along.

'What a lovely baby,' the nurse said, rocking the pillow. She giggled a little, saving this story for the next time she met Rita.

The woman narrowed her eyes. 'Why are you laughing like an idiot?'

The nurse had gotten used to this too. The sudden hurtful statements that were hurled her way.

'I laugh when I want to. You have a problem?'

'Yes. I do, actually,' said the woman, turning her face away.

'Oh, that doesn't matter,' the nurse replied, cupping the woman's chin with one hand cajolingly. 'You will get over it.'

The nurse was enjoying herself. When the woman got imperious and hoity-toity she would sometimes take a few petty digs at her. In this room, she didn't swallow her pride like she used to with the vicious classist patients at the hospital, where answering back could have cost her the job.

On some days the two of them enjoyed a sort of companionship that was equal and calming. The nurse would read from the Upanishads or tell the woman stories from her own childhood. She would listen, ask questions, and such days would pass peacefully enough.

'What is the qualification required for studying nursing?' the woman asked on a day when she knew the nurse was her nurse and she was the patient. A day on which she had made her peace with that reality and didn't fuss or rant.

'Class twelve you have to pass, then you can study nursing. It's hard, though. I almost gave up many times,' said the nurse. 'The work can be back-breaking. The bedpans, setting up home ICUs, dealing with patients, keeping vigil at night.'

'I would like to be a nurse. Is it too late for that, for me?' the woman asked, and the nurse sighed. It had been a good day but the sun was setting, all cotton wool and egg yolk. And the woman's mind with it, leaving her at the threshold of impossible wishes that harmed no one – till night came to drown the mind in darkness, both known and unknown, dangerous and safe, in turn.

'Not too late for anything,' said the nurse in a placatory, sing-song voice. But that voice never worked. The woman sniffed at being talked down to, pursed her lips and demanded the nurse keep quiet; she had no time for her nonsense. Still, the nurse didn't mind. She had worked in households where the family had been demanding, asking for reports every day, checking the patient's hygiene, nagging and scolding. The pay was good but the way families treated nurses could be crap.

In this house no one interfered with the caregiving. The doctor came in once every ten days, checked the medicines and the patient's health. He would know if she wasn't doing her job properly, but it wasn't fear that made the nurse take her job seriously. She was conscientious, god-fearing, with a sense of responsibility. And the older son, though he met his mother rarely, did do his duty in a detached manner that suited her.

She reported to his study every Friday evening – told him if there were any problems, if the woman needed new clothes or cosmetics or medicines. It was a system that worked quite flawlessly or so it seemed. But things could change and they inevitably would. It was hardly the nurse's fault. What was written would happen and that was that.

the woman who left

Vasundhara was feeling much better as she applied for the e-pass for inter-state travel on her laptop. She had a sense of purpose now, had decided on a course of action. Mukul had said he would go with her. They also needed an e-pass for Shalini for the return journey. Her cousin, who was a senior bureaucrat and helping her get the passes on a priority basis, had suggested they get just the one for Shalini, so she could make her way on her own. It was a preposterous suggestion. How would Shalini come by herself? Who would bring her? Finally, they settled on getting three passes. She was happy that Mukul had so readily agreed to come with her, though she could tell he was confused by her vague, unfounded worries about Shalini. He seemed to have no idea what Shalini was capable of, and it was best that it stayed that way.

Despite his unease, he hadn't questioned what she wanted to save Shalini from nor would she have said if he had. In any case, Vasundhara was acting instinctively with no idea of what was to come. How could she prepare to avoid a calamity that had not taken shape yet, that hung so flimsily on a framework of memories?

Mukul was charming, sensible, and the right person for someone like her daughter. They had spent some very pleasant evenings together, the three of them. Her heart had sunk when Shalini had announced, a month or so back, that she was going to the hills to meet Akshar.

Vasundhara remembered the first time she had met him when she had gone to drop Shalini off at boarding school. As soon as they entered the school grounds, Shalini's face had lit up. It had pleased Vasundhara to see that her daughter was at long last well-adjusted in a place that she loved. But then it wasn't really the school so much. Little Shalini couldn't wait to be with her best friend again. Which should have been endearing but … Vasundhara wasn't able to account for her own wariness when it came to that boy.

Long years ago, she had decided to send her daughter to boarding school after the incident that led to Adil leaving and it was not a decision she had ever regretted. She was at her wits' end, the child psychiatrist wasn't of much help either, nor was her ex-husband or his parents. Everyone had tried. But nothing had worked.

Akshar had been a lifeline, giving the little girl something precious that kept her afloat, that made her want to be the best she could be – just for his sake. If Vasundhara was honest she would have to admit that his presence had been life-changing. The morbid, inflexible, neurotic child had grown into a teenager who was difficult but not impossible, and an adult who was sorted and pleasant or so it appeared.

The love Shalini bore Akshar was obsessive and permanent. When she had started dating like other young people her age, Vasundhara had been relieved. Yet she sensed her daughter had simply reconciled to the fact that Akshar was not romantically interested in her. Her eyes never lit up; her face never became soft as mush when she spoke about any person apart from Akshar. Mukul was the first boyfriend that Vasundhara had felt might develop into something more lasting. But then Akshar had surfaced after a long hiatus, beckoned her to the hills, and off she had gone, with not a glance backwards.

If only the lockdown had been announced a day later Shalini would have been safely home. And now there she was. Sounding unhinged on the phone. Uncertain, hysterical, garbled. Vasundhara needed to get her little girl home. As soon as possible.

the woman who was unafraid of fire

I slept well that night. There were footsteps outside my door again, but they no longer bothered me. I had a deep, long sleep that made up for the many sleepless nights I'd spent on that bed. When I woke up, I thought at first that it was still night, or at best pre-dawn. Mornings here were redemption, the best and sanest part of each day – the soft leaves outside my window, the rolling hills, the wispy clouds, the sunlit patterns on the walls. However, today my room was sunk in a ghoulish blue subterranean haze. The dark contours of the branches outside my window were rolling from side to side like drunken creatures, and I could hear their groans as whiplashes of rain beat down with little mercy. I checked my phone – it was 8:30 a.m. Akshar must have already gone to the hospital. The sun had clearly abandoned the skies on the day there was going to be a burial in the woods.

I got ready to meet the day. The corridors had a musty smell that wasn't pleasant, as if the sewage pipes had broken with the onslaught of rain and wind. Near the staircase there was a wet patch on which I slipped. The ceiling, tired and old, was leaking. A drop fell on me, and I wondered if I should get the bucket from my bathroom and place it there. Or I could just let Ravinder know. The aristocratic lifestyle was suiting me, it seemed – I was getting quite used to directing the staff rather than taking care of things on my own.

For once Ravinder didn't greet me with sullen resentment. He was anxious. 'Saab went to the hospital. Two hours back. Can you phone him and ask if Aahana baby is alright?' His unquestioning, submissive love for Akshar and Aahana – a habit of generations. Ravinder's father and grandfather had served Akshar's family too. His children were the first to have left this household. Who would they have served if they had stayed back in this house on the verge of extinction?

I didn't really want to call Akshar, and not just because of what had happened on the staircase last night. Chances were, it wasn't weighing on his mind the way it was on mine. 'You know how your Saab is – doesn't like to be disturbed. He will call if he has anything to say.' This was true, and Ravinder nodded.

I had black coffee and some biscuits. Ravinder offered to get toast and eggs but I was anxious and restless. There was a tight knot in my stomach that I was sure wouldn't move to make place for food. My phone rang. I saw Mukul's name on the screen, as if from another lifetime, and hesitated. I was too distraught to string together coherent thoughts, to align words into neat lines. But I felt so alone that I wanted to hear Mukul's voice, be calmed by his measured manner of speaking.

'The lockdown's being extended,' he said.

'How long have I been here?' I'd lost track of dates.

'What do you mean?' Mukul asked sharply. 'Do you even *want* to return? I spoke to your mother yesterday. We have applied for e-passes for inter-state travel. Using whatever contacts we have, it should get done today. The lockdown is absolute with no sign of lifting.'

I went and sat on the porch outside the dining room. The rain had slowed to a drizzle, but it was a dark and dreary day. Mukul asked me to finish some work, create a video for a client and send it across by tomorrow. I knew he was trying to keep me busy, and I knew I wouldn't do it. It would be like playing office-office while the world ended. He didn't know about the dead baby, the burial, and I couldn't get myself to talk about any of it.

I wasn't sure how long I sat out there. Till Savita, all weeping and distressed, came to call me. Saab had returned.

Akshar was standing in the driveway. He was cradling a small white bundle in his arms. It seemed he had aged in the last few hours, the weight of that tiny bundle causing his whole body to sag – the shine in his eyes was gone, the bags under them prominent. The sky was still grey and heavy; at least it wasn't raining. I could hear my heart hammering in my chest as if I'd run a marathon. I don't know quite what I'd expected but the sight of that incredibly small cloth-wrapped form in Akshar's arms was beyond heartbreaking. I wasn't a parent and didn't ever want to be one, yet there was something in that moment that was pure and beyond cynicism.

The dark theorist of the last few weeks was, for now at least, a man grappling with a grief as large as the cosmic horror he had anticipated. I expected Akshar to take the baby to the burial ground straight away, but he headed into the house. He wants to visit his mother, was my first thought, but that wasn't the case. He took the shrouded baby to his study. Perhaps because it was his happy place. The bookshelves with pages and pages containing all the worlds and words he loved. Ravinder brought him a cup of strong tulsi chai. Akshar didn't put the precious bundle down. He shifted it gently to the crook of his left arm and took a sip of tea.

'It is all for the best, Shalini, but … this. I'm feeling …?' The tears were streaming down his face. I went up to him, put an arm around his shoulders and rubbed my cheek against his. I could feel his rough, salty tears against my skin. I had no words, and he expected none. Akshar got up when he finished his tea, rocking the bundle gently as if putting the baby to sleep, and we went outside. I wondered where Sahil was; I hadn't seen him in days.

It had started drizzling again, but that seemed like an inconsequential detail. Akshar led the way to the back of his mansion, where the trees and plants were wild, tangled and endless. I was a few steps behind him, and Ravinder and his wife followed – a dismal procession headed into the forest on the hills.

Akshar stopped when we were near the gardener's hut. He was already waiting outside with a shovel in his hand. In the darkness of the stormy day, I couldn't quite identify him – the forest was alive with strange, amorphous life forms today, humans and others melding into each other. The gardener didn't speak, just started walking, and we followed him down a fairly steep slope to a clearing where in the muddy, brown earth he had dug a heartstoppingly tiny grave. We formed a circle around this piece of dug-out soil. It was dry, the little grave, untouched by the rain. The leaves and branches of the surrounding trees had formed a protective canopy over it.

Akshar's face was cast in stone now. Not sorrowful anymore. His lips were moving, though I couldn't hear what he was saying. Perhaps he was chanting some forgotten mantra that resided somewhere deep inside him. I averted my eyes every time they fell on the shrouded baby in his arms. The face was covered and the white cloth neatly wrapped around the body; it looked like an elongated parcel that had come in the post, the sort for which the shape doesn't immediately give away what is inside.

He went down on his knees in the damp mud, kissed the precious bundle tenderly and held on to it so close that for a moment I thought he wouldn't know how to let go. But then he bent down, lowered the sleeping baby into its waiting cradle and touched his forehead to the ground, curling into himself in a fetal position from which he didn't get up for a while. I saw that the mali, Ravinder, Savita, Jai Singh and his family (I hadn't noticed them join us) were all kneeling on the ground too, in a circle behind us. I remained standing. Akshar took a handful of mud and placed it in the grave, gently. He turned to look at the mali, who just nodded. Akshar got up and without a backward glance, walked away.

I had no idea if he was following any established ritual or had just created his own, but I turned to follow Akshar back to the house. None of the rest moved. They were still kneeling as if in a nativity play, paying homage to an unknown spirit that only they knew about. Akshar and his staff seemed to be part of a larger network of sorrow to which I didn't belong.

Akshar was walking fast. Soon I couldn't see him anymore but I knew my way back. I longed for the dappled sunshine under the trees that had made these hilly treks so beautiful on other days.

Though the trees had largely protected us from the drizzle, I was soaking wet by now. I would have to go up to my room and change. As I passed Akshar's study, I noticed the door was ajar with a column of thin light spilling out.

He was sitting at his desk, back rigidly straight, with his hands steepled in front of his face, as if at a board meeting of some sort. He nodded at me and gestured at the chair opposite him. I didn't say I was cold and wet and wanted to go and change my clothes. I just went and huddled miserably in front of him. He had switched on the red metal office lamp on his desk, which, instead of making the room brighter, gave a sinister sheen to the wooden floor. The wall lights were shut, as was the window behind him.

For a while he didn't speak. I don't know what I was expecting. Sorrow and grief possibly but what I got was what I'd been getting for the last ten days or so. Perhaps it was easier for him that way. To distance himself from the pain of loss with the jargon of existential horror. But it wasn't easy for me, sitting in my uncomfortably wet clothes. I felt a sense of spine-chilling horror that I'd not experienced till then as I listened to Akshar talk in a low monotone. At one point he read aloud from one of his innumerable books. I knew these were not his words but that made it worse. The cold articulation by an author in America in a different era that echoed convincingly in a small study in an inconsequential hill station in India. It made me feel breathless, encapsulated by the terror that Akshar was spelling out, enunciating beautifully, as if reading to a spellbound theatre audience:

> I hear them buzzing like flies in the blackness … they are struggling, straining every second to keep the sky above them, to keep the sun in the sky, to keep the dead in the earth – to keep all things, so to speak, *where they belong* … Is it any wonder that they are all tempted by a universal vice, that in some dark street of the mind a soft voice whispers to one and all: 'Lay down your burden.' Then thoughts begin to drift, a mystical magnetism pulls them this way and that, faces start to change.

Akshar looked up from the page and said in a voice that was overcome with awe, 'Ligotti. Isn't he amazing? This is how it was. I could hear them struggling, I was struggling myself, with my personal loss. I felt sorrow of a kind I'd never experienced before but then I heard that whisper: Lay down your burden, it said. Just like I read out now. And I did.'

Akshar put the book away and continued to talk. I wasn't listening. I was back on the mall road, taking tentative steps towards the fire from which he had pulled me away. Lay down your burden, it had said, in the exact same voice in which Akshar had read out those lines just now, and that's when I'd taken the first step forward.

The faces in the fire had begun to change – Akshar's baby face from our school days mutated, the wrinkles grew, the skin sagged, till he was older than his mother was today.

I shook my head to rid myself of that voice, of that image. I tried to listen to what Akshar was saying. Slowly, clearly. 'There is nothing out there. For a moment I was fooled. I was crushed by sorrow, by love, my child, my only child … but I know now, I know none of it is true at all. It's a void, a beautiful void. The burnings. Towns swallowed by fire.'

I tried to tune out his words, to get away. But it was impossible. I was drawn to Akshar's obsessive, bewildering monologue – *shama-parwana*. When he paused for breath I asked, in a desperate rush to distract myself and him, 'But how is Aahana doing? Did you meet her in the morning?'

'I did see her unconscious form on the hospital bed,' Akshar said. His tone was matter-of-fact, neutral; his eyes were lifeless. In this moment everything seemed to have been swallowed by the mist and darkness of the void that Akshar and I knew so well. There were clouds and fog in my brain. I could no longer think clearly.

In an attempt to tether myself to the real world I read the latest news reports online. There were trackers and updates every minute, articles being spun out by writers predicting doom. There were also those who foresaw redemption of sorts – the burnings as a trigger warning from an environment that was crying for help, one that would lead to improvement in the future. Ecological information, solutions, measures that we needed to take. But none of it was definitive, no one really knew what was going on.

The optimistic thought the fires meant nothing at all; they would be the first to go. They didn't believe in being careful on the streets; they rushed around as always. Not that it mattered. Even the careful were only delaying the inevitable. The fires would have fun hunting down those who resisted, those who shut themselves into their houses and went slowly mad, or who walked carefully down the streets, always an eye out for a fire that might break out. Those people made the fires smile, the flames burn brighter. We'll be back for you later, they thought, and decided to finish off the easier sort of people first.

I was ostensibly working in my room. I needed to get a grip. I was beginning to morph into Akshar, mirroring his morbid, fanciful ideas of fury and destruction. After lunch I had told him I needed to finish off some work for a client. I don't know if he heard, but he did nod. It was clear that he hadn't slept since the burial yesterday – his eyes were hollow, his hair uncombed, his skin so pale and translucent. The constant presence of Akshar befuddled my senses – my mind was turbulent, moving in every direction and yet completely still, like the apparent racing of railway tracks from the window of a train compartment. I used to love that as a child: how the stationary tracks, flashing silver, appeared to move at breakneck speed.

Mukul called. He sounded impatient. I was sitting on the bed with my laptop, gazing out at a sky that was calm today, not raging anymore, now that the burial was done.

'We are getting the passes. They should be ready in a day or two. Your mom and I will drive down to get you.'

'Oh, you'll come all the way, for me?' I asked wonderingly. 'With my mother?'

'Well, yes, that can't be helped, Shalini.' I couldn't gauge his tone, whether he was being facetious or angry. 'It's your mother. She's really worried. I don't understand … anyway, we will come. We'll just have to be very careful while driving and hope for the best.'

My mother did call often. I told her I was coping, that I was fine enough under the circumstances. Perhaps she and Mukul were right. I might feel better at home, though how could I abandon Akshar? I'd done many awful things in my life but one thing I'd never done was leave Akshar when he needed me.

After an hour or two of futile stabs at work I gave up all pretence of it. I decided to go for a walk before the sun dropped between the hills. It was still all golden and beautiful outside. As I reached the staircase, I met the nurse coming down the corridor.

'The last couple of days … sorry, I did mean to drop by,' I said. As I stood there dithering, the door to

Akshar's mother's room opened, and suddenly there she was, floating down the corridor, tall and wraith-like in the now-familiar full-sleeved nightgown, her grey-white hair flowing down her back.

'I want to see the walls.' She looked at the nurse and then at me.

'Yes, yes, we can go and look at them,' replied the nurse, nodding. And explained to me, 'She was an artist. So many paintings. They are in a room downstairs. Sometimes we go and look at them.'

The three of us headed towards the staircase. 'You will see the walls too?' Akshar's mother asked me eagerly.

'She doesn't remember that they are called paintings. Keeps calling them walls,' the nurse said. 'Come with us? God knows she gets to meet no one but me all the time. And yes, Sahil, he comes every day. That makes her happy.'

I had almost forgotten Sahil was in the house. He clearly stayed out of his brother's way. It was a large enough mansion to get lost in if one wished. The nurse turned left on the first floor, which I hadn't been to at all. The corridor was darker than ours; there was a singular naked bulb at one end. The nurse drew back the bolt in the penultimate room, at the opposite end of the corridor. It slid back easily. It seemed that the door was opened often enough.

The room reminded me of the one in which Akshar had been sitting the first day when I'd arrived. It had the same long, narrow, pointed windows with dusty maroon velvet drapes that were set at a great height. Some slivers of sunlight from these strange dysfunctional windows fell here and there but most of the room was shrouded in darkness, till the nurse turned on the light switch. There were three massive chandeliers of frosted glass hanging down from the vaulted ceilings and they all lit up, flooding the room with light. The paint was peeling from the pistachio walls, the lackluster marble floor had cracks in which dirt had accumulated but that didn't take away from the air of medieval grandeur. It was only when the light fell on the walls that I saw the paintings.

I was surprised at how many there were – it was like being in an art gallery. Huge framed canvases. The first one to catch my eye was a massive oil painting with a faded black mansion dimly visible in the background, almost like a watermark. In front of it, vivid and bright, were these saffron, turmeric and scarlet flames, clustered into a lotus-like shape. Small slits revealed large terrified eyes trapped behind the flames, the slender, jewelled neck and profile of a woman. It was arresting and eerie. My eyes scanned the room, my senses flooding with the colours and images, my head beginning to hurt as if I had been staring at a kaleidoscope of psychedelic patterns for hours. I felt fear and loathing flood my every pore. For a moment. Then the feeling was gone. 'You did these?' I asked Akshar's mother.

'Yes, my hands and fingers,' she replied. The nurse and I looked at each other and laughed. I fleetingly wondered why I had felt such a sense of deep fear a minute back. Disha Gupta frowned with the precociousness of a child who knows she is being laughed at and doesn't like it, and added, 'Oils and turpentine.'

One did not need to be a patron to see that these were mature, gorgeous works of art. I went around the room quickly at first, without registering much beyond the vibrant colours and flamboyant strokes. Heavy, grand, ominous, and the theme that unequivocally ran through them was of fire. I swallowed and my throat felt constricted, like a fish bone was stuck in it.

The paintings had been placed chronologically, tracing the artist's life. The first painting was of a young couple, dancing close and tight, in the first flush of love. It was probably a scene from a party that was thrown for the newlyweds, Avyukt and Disha Gupta. The man's hands rested lightly on the woman's lower back, while hers were placed on his broad shoulders. A fireplace behind them glowed softly. The second painting was different in character. It was a bird's-eye view of a town, full of minute details. The hills, cottages, people going about their lives, a cascading river and pretty little fires everywhere. I imagined Disha Gupta creating this one when she was still new to this hill station, when she still romanticized it as her aristocratic husband's birthplace to which she had come as a young bright-eyed bride.

The third painting was ambivalent; I couldn't gauge its mood. Long shadows of a man and a woman under a tree, a strange greyish red. The colours of a dying fire, partially ashen. The tree was exquisite, every emerald leaf distinct. There were round, blood-red fruits on the branches. The brightness of the tree made the shadows under it more stark and darkly attractive. As I went around the room, the paintings progressively lost colour and the lightness of touch but the suggestion of fire and ashes remained. There was one of a mother and child walking up a sloping mountain road – towards a half-lit fire at the top of the hill.

Another one showed the local women sitting in a circle around a dying fire, exactly the way they had been the other day when Akshar and I'd gone for a walk. Eyes deepened with kohl, dry deathly pale lips that looked like they'd been stitched together with white thread, heavy jewellery and lavishly embroidered shawls worn like turbans on their heads, their faces stricken, heavy with loss.

The mood in the remaining paintings was sombre; the colours shifted to browns and greys, the turquoise blues and fluorescent greens and sunshine yellows were long gone, as if some tubes of paint had been stolen from her art supplies and never replaced. The paintings were grim and desperate till I came to the last two. I stood still, a sense of horror slowly coming over me. Paintings she would have done before she got Alzheimer's – projections into a future that was already fading for her.

One was a big portrait of Aahana, recognizable to anyone who had met her. Her face wore a pensive, angelic half-smile and her skin was transparent below her flimsy strappy dress. Inside her huge and swollen tummy could be seen a curled up baby, not so much a foetus as a newborn wrapped in a white sheet, resting on a bed of glowing coals. Aahana was standing straight but her body, stomach downwards, was buried deep inside the earth, and the earth was a molten mass of flames and fire, burning red and muddy at the same time. I shuddered. The baby that was declared dead before it was born. And the earth all aflame, as it was today. I wondered if Akshar had seen this painting, if it had always resided in some corner of his subconscious, guiding him to prophesize the death of his own son before he even came into the world. I put my hand on my stomach, which felt hot and clammy.

Akshar's mother was standing right next to me as I stared at the painting. On her face was a look of cunning that made my heart stop for a moment. She and I, we recognized each other. I moved a few steps away from her. Suddenly I couldn't bear to be so near her; she was no longer the confused forgotten woman who was lost to the world – there was an immensity of knowing in her eyes. She knew me, she saw herself in me, that was why she liked me. I felt a deep sense of dread. Yes, I could tell her a thing or two about playing with fire, couldn't I? Taking a few more steps away from her, I found myself in front of the last canvas.

The painting was of this mansion, and it captured the sense of disquiet I felt within it. There were small reptilian shapes crouching on the walls, creeping and repulsive. The sky was dark and stormy and there were these strange orange-yellow tongues, like little flames, that were licking at the reptiles. And right down the middle of the painting there was a streak of lightning and fire, which split the house into two. The two sides of the silvery-red stripe weren't aligned. The house appeared surreal and misshapen and on the verge of collapse.

I turned to the nurse to find her staring intently at the painting of Aahana. She looked nervous all of a sudden. 'I didn't, I don't know ...' she was stammering. I couldn't quite bring myself to care what she knew or didn't. I remembered Mukul saying that he and my mother would be here to get me in a few days. I tried to hold on to that thought. I need to get away from this malodorous mansion and its inhabitants before the walls sucked me in and the corridors spat me out, forcing me to act in ways that I didn't want.

I loved Akshar, I could never harm him. My mind went back to that night in the Andamans. I remembered watching my mother and Adil in the throes of an orgasm. I was a child again. I saw myself standing there, a matchbox in my hand. It had to be fire. It always had to be fire. Nothing but fire could cleanse. I couldn't stop thinking of Adil, of my mother's many lovers, and the acrid smell of fire and ashes. This mansion exuded vileness but it belonged to Akshar, he whom I would always protect.

I had a splitting headache, like strange little fireworks going off inside my brain – neurological shockwaves of pain that numbed all else. Like the ones I'd suffered ever since I was a child. My stomach hurt too. Searing pain that came and receded in waves. I had a vision of curling into myself like a snail, coils and layers that insulated feelings and thoughts, lulled into a safe circle of peace.

'Aahana will be here tomorrow,' Akshar said when I made my way to his study at last. *Aahana will be here tomorrow* – a line I had also heard on the first evening after I'd reached this godforsaken mansion. 'She will stay with us from now on.'

The fireworks in my brain were noisy and distracting. 'I'm feeling so unwell, Akshar. I need to get some rest.'

Akshar nodded. He didn't ask why I had come all the way down if I was unwell. I went upstairs slowly but once I reached my room, the pain in my stomach was unbearable. I ran to the bathroom, puked buckets and felt marginally better. I lay down on the bed, though I knew I wouldn't be able to sleep even as my body craved a blackout that would drown all that was buzzing inside my head – paintings, Adil, my mother and these insane neurological fireworks.

I didn't notice when the footsteps started. If it was a minute later or many hours. At first I mistook it for the pounding in my head. But it was unmistakable really – padded, quick, numerous. I felt the unknown entity pushing against my bedroom door: knocking, turning the handle. The air in the room thickened, it was red-hot in a way that was almost joyous, like *gulal* scattering everywhere. My breath was coming in shallow, quick bursts. I was unable to draw in a lungful of air. The footsteps were echoing the hammering in my head; they were everywhere, inside, outside.

It was then that I heard the women chanting. Just like on the hillside that day. Deep reverberations. Resounding, echoing, the chants wafted in through the open window. I still couldn't take full deep breaths but I was calmed, cocooned by light and beauty. I felt deep sleep descending like a cloud upon me. It was a relief. I sank into that cloud of sleep and let it claim me. The footsteps receded. Mercy was at hand. I fell asleep, or perhaps unconscious. I don't know which and it hardly mattered.

9

the woman in the room

When Akshar had finished school there was a graduation ceremony. Avyukt and Disha Gupta had attended – probably the last parental duty they fulfilled as a couple. There were two memories that lingered with Disha after the ceremony. One was of little Shalini, bright-eyed and cheering fervently every time Akshar went up on stage to get an award. She had wondered at her son's ability to garner this sort of unquestioning devotion. From Aahana in the hills and Shalini at the school.

The other memory was of Shalini's mother, Vasundhara. Instinctively, the two women had liked each other. They hadn't discussed their children at all; they had left that to the fathers. Disha had been able to tell that Vasundhara's relationship with her own daughter was strained, just like hers with her son. Typically, it was fathers who weren't good at parenting, but both Akshar and Shalini belonged to their dads.

Disha had noticed Vasundhara didn't like her son. Perhaps because of how dominant he was in her daughter's life, how she planned her life around him while he loved her back but sparingly and at his own will.

Those memories were gone now. They were too unimportant, too thin, to remain. Yet the woman in the room had felt a glimmer when she met Shalini. She wasn't the other girl. The woman disliked the other girl, always had. She had loved Meher, for a while, the girl's mother. It had upset Disha when Meher, her only friend in the hills, grew slowly distant. Of course she later realized that the more Meher loved Avyukt, the less she loved his wife. That was fair. Meher must have felt torn, unsure. Giving birth to Avyukt's child must have messed her up further. After the babies, half-twins, were born, the two women drifted further apart, never met again except by chance.

Meher did come to visit the woman in the room. Once every few months. It wasn't meant to be an apology, or some perverted penance of sorts. She simply felt the desire to meet Disha sometimes. Though the visits upset her more than anything. To meet Disha who was no longer Disha. To be in the house of her dead lover whom she had loved more than his wife ever managed to. The last time she had visited was in mid-March, when the fires were becoming more common in India.

'We made a mess of our lives, didn't we, Disha?' she had said to her old friend, knowing she couldn't reach her. 'And now our children, they are suffering.'

'*Haisha-hoisha*, we all fall down,' Disha Gupta had replied. Which was appropriate, decided Meher. Everything was and always had been falling down as far as their families were concerned. The irony of it after all these years was that they were both going to be grandmothers to the same baby. Incest. Exactly what they had all struggled to avoid, but here it was. The sins of the father and all that. Meher had wondered how it would all end.

'Haisha-hoisha, we all fall down,' Disha had said again. Well, yes, a plague, a fire – bodies aflame, skin peeling, impossible heat. Fire was said to purify. Who or what exactly it purified Meher hadn't known. Nor had she cared to know; she had been long past notions of morality and purification, and all the hypocrisies they implied.

the woman who left

The roads were empty in a way that would have been unimaginable before the age of the fires, smooth roads stretching to infinity. The first fire Mukul and Vasundhara had encountered was soon after leaving. She had sensed the blaze from a mile away and asked Mukul to slow down, keep to the left. It was unreal, like a video game. Keenness, muscle memory, alert reflexes – you needed all of those to not self-destruct. But how long could you evade the punishing flame? That was the question.

Vasundhara knew how to be safe from fire, she had way too much experience in that department. She alerted Mukul in advance and a couple of times they pulled up on the side and waited for the fire to spend its force. On empty streets the fires never lasted, it seemed they needed traffic and humans to gain strength, to cause destruction.

'Let me know if you want a break. I can drive for a bit,' said Vasundhara.

'I'll drive and you do the fire spotting. I don't see them coming the way you do,' he replied.

Vasundhara thought of Shalini as a child, lighting match after match till the box was empty and there was a pile of charred matchsticks on the floor. Then came the fire in the house, everything up in flames, both she and Adil in hospital. Adil had had to undergo cosmetic surgery on his arms and chest. While he was in the ICU Vasundhara had known she would lose him. Even if he lived. It was inevitable. After, he had never said he blamed her and he didn't. It was just that he couldn't live with them anymore. It was understandable.

In her dreams every night for many years she saw Shalini standing at the foot of their bed, a small girl with tangled hair and blank staring eyes, the dark circles under them enormous. Exactly like it had happened. The fire had caught on so fast that when she woke up, the sheets, satin and slippery, were already up in flames. It was Adil's side of the bed that had caught fire. He had lost consciousness as she tried to douse the flames, rolling the bedcover over him and the burning sheet, beating them with her hands before she collapsed, too.

Her head spinning and light, the room thick with smoke, she had seen little Shalini, still transfixed near the foot of the bed, and in her hands a matchbox. The little girl had told her mother later, when they were back from the hospital, that she was lighting matches and one had slipped and fallen on the satin sheets. She had come to her mother's room because she couldn't fall asleep. Shalini hadn't wept or shown remorse even once. Her face had been carved in stone, her tongue darted in and out of her mouth to wet cracked, dry lips. The police, the doctor had all concluded the child was in shock. It was trauma, deep and horrible.

Adil left for the Andamans soon after he was out of the hospital. His beautiful face was marred with an ugly, long scar that stretched from his right eye to his chin, his body patched with skin grafts, still healing from third-degree burns. On the staircase, with a suitcase in one hand, he had hugged Vasundhara and said he wished he could have done better by her. She had remained dry-eyed.

'We will be in touch,' he had said. She had said yes but known it wouldn't be the case. That part of her life was over. Adil had been her weakness, she had to let him go. She had left her husband for Adil, though it wasn't just that. There were other reasons. Reasons that were about herself. She needed to live with herself before she lived with anyone else again.

And then there was Shalini. Vasundhara had refused to blame herself for what was wrong in the child. But she had to do something about it. When the boarding school idea was floated, she had been relieved. Sending Shalini away would mean that she wouldn't have to come home every evening and face those beady eyes. That was when she had felt guilty for the first time. The flood of relief at the idea of not having to see her daughter every day.

Yet it did make all the difference. Vasundhara had learnt to relax, to enjoy her job, to have a life of her own. And for the summer and winter vacations the child was back, sometimes with her and sometimes with her dad in Singapore. It wasn't as hard as it used to be. They even, very slowly over the years, learnt to talk to each other. They could never be close – there wasn't enough trust – but it was what it was. An uneasy truce that worked most of the time. Except for brief periods of silence, sometimes days, sometimes weeks.

All else healed but the embers of that fire never left. And whenever there was a hint that Shalini was in trouble, those embers glowed and Vasundhara couldn't rest till she smothered them and started life again.

The fires raging all over the world today brought back too much. She remembered her own screams as she woke up that night to find her bed ablaze and Adil unconscious beside her. And the little girl. Just standing and staring, mesmerized by the flames, the shadow of a smile on her pasty face.

the woman who was unafraid of fire

When we were ten, Akshar had received a letter from his mother that made him cry. I could remember lying with my head on Jugaad's long, sleek back in the school lawns. Akshar had blown his nose on the sleeve of his blazer so there were little white streaks on the dark blue fabric near his armpit. Akshar used to cry often till he was ten or so. After that he suddenly manned up. I think that summer his father gave him a pep talk on how boys didn't cry.

'I hate my mother. She says I can't spend the holidays at home. We are going to London to meet my grandparents,' he had said. To me it had sounded wonderful. A vacation in London. But I had dutifully commiserated. I knew how much Akshar loved his hills, his home, his Aahana.

'Why doesn't Aahana come to our school?' Not that I wanted her to. At all.

'She likes her school. It's a really good school. If it wasn't only for girls I would have studied there too.' I had felt a familiar stab of jealousy. I was already used to it by then; it came and went without upsetting me unduly. So easily he imagined himself with Aahana. And when he did, I ceased to matter. I had hugged Jugaad. I came first with him. Not that Akshar minded but everyone knew I was Jugaad's first love.

This random memory had come back to me because of Akshar's mother's paintings. Along with that letter, Akshar's mother had sent a sketch of the Big Ben where the clock's hands were replaced with gnarled hairy claws. She often used to send him little ink sketches, which he would show me. Sometimes just sketches with no accompanying letter. He didn't like them and nor did I. Dark, dismal sketches, of a leopard eating a hyena, of a crocodile under a bed on which a child was peacefully sleeping – enough to give us nightmares. Cruel, unthinking drawings to send to a son who was away at boarding school.

One of the drawings she had sent Akshar in school had been of a delicate little doll's house inside a fireplace, going up in flames. I remembered that sketch as I thought about those large canvases in the art gallery, especially the one of this very mansion catching fire, with reptilian shapes inside the walls. I was instinctively drawn to a person with an affinity for fire, like Akshar's mother. Someone like Akshar, despite his end-of-the-world theories, didn't really know anything about fire – how powerful, how pure, how transcendental it could be. I remembered Jugaad dying in the fire and that was one of the hardest days of my life but I knew Akshar had nothing to do with it. Perhaps Sahil. Now that I knew about the mother it seemed plausible.

I was standing at the window of my room. The mad headache and visions of last night had been washed away by sleep. Fitful and uneasy sleep but still. My mother had called a little while back to say she and Mukul were on their way. That they would be here early tomorrow morning, if not tonight. It was a long drive but they didn't plan to make too many stops. In any case everything was shut. No roadside dhabas or hotels were open, the traffic on the highway close to nil.

I packed my suitcase and made my way down to tell Akshar I would be leaving. He just nodded when I said my mom and Mukul were on their way. He was waiting for Aahana, I assumed, from the way he kept looking out at the driveway from the window of his study.

'You said yesterday that Aahana is coming to stay. Indefinitely?' I asked. Aahana was going to be here, and Akshar wouldn't need me anymore.

'Yes, Reyhan doesn't want her in his house. She could have gone back to her parents of course, but I told her to come here till I'm unable to take care of her or myself anymore. It's only a matter of time.'

I could believe that. He looked skeletal and haggard. A car pulled up in the driveway. Akshar said, 'Oh good, he's here.'

'He?'

'Rana Mahajan,' Akshar replied. 'I need to instruct him on the changes to the will.'

The reason why I'd come here in the first place. For a trust deed that was now redundant. The days had been passing so slowly yet so much had transpired. Lives turned upside down by death.

'But don't you believe the world is ending, Akshar?' I asked. 'Why bother?'

'It might take a while – two, three, four years. In the meantime, people will lose jobs, income. As far as possible I want to make sure those who have loved me, cared for me, don't suffer privation. Ravinder, Jai Singh and his family. Aahana, you.'

It bothered me that Akshar repeatedly called us those who had loved him, those who had cared for him

– without giving any hint of his having loved us back. Since he couldn't give us love in return, he would provide money. Except with Aahana, which was a relationship that existed outside the framework of transaction, the only one that was based on reciprocity. I tried to push back my old hatred for Aahana which suddenly leapt up my throat. I wanted to vomit it out, the putrid, awful hate that lay buried deep inside me; I was tired of swallowing it. I kept convincing myself it wasn't there anymore and then in unguarded moments like this it surged through me, painful, angry. But every time, I would banish it again. I prided myself on at least being able to do that. It didn't break me, it made me stronger.

I greeted Rana when he entered the room. He looked lost, perhaps unsure of what was expected of him. I said I would take a walk and left them to talk business. Akshar had lost his newborn child, his lover was being thrown out by her husband, his head was buzzing with apocalyptic theories. That the practical need to keep his finances in order was still important to Akshar was impressive.

I turned left when I reached the driveway and onto one of the walking trails at the back of the mansion. Today was a day of light and sun. I could hear birds chirping, the leaves were glistening and freshly scrubbed from the recent bath. I went past the gardener's cottage and down a steep slope to the clearing where, below a canopy formed by a circle of trees, lay the little rectangular mound of fresh earth under which Aahana and Akshar's baby was buried. Someone had placed white flowers and leaves on the tiny grave. Flowers for a baby who hadn't lived to ever see one.

The meaninglessness of our existence was a small comfort; there was peace in knowing nothing mattered, that it was all falling apart like it was always meant to. After some time, the earth next to me shifted and Akshar was suddenly there, sitting beside me. He put his arm around my shoulders. We sat together, close, for a long, long time. We didn't speak at all. I rested my head on his shoulder. These were some of our last moments of togetherness before I left. Our last few moments of togetherness on this earth.

It was after a while that I asked, 'Won't Aahana be coming soon? Shouldn't we go back?'

'Yes,' said Akshar. 'I want you to know something, Shalini. You've always been here for me. You didn't come second. I know I've taken you for granted but it doesn't mean that I don't know.'

I felt a lump in my throat. I didn't believe him at all – trusting did not come easily to me – but I liked what he was trying to say. I wanted him to spell it out so I would have tangible words to hold on to and remember. 'Know what, Akshar?'

'That you've resented my relationship with Aahana since we were kids and perhaps rightly so. That you've often found me self-obsessed and insensitive.'

I got up. That was enough. I bent down and pinched his cheeks like he was a child. 'Yes, self-obsessed, insensitive and uncaring. But I'll always love you, Akshar. You will always come first, don't worry.'

'Even when I'm gone?' he asked eagerly, and I felt tears spring to my eyes. After all this time, after all that had happened, that still mattered to Akshar. He had to come first forever.

'Yes, wherever you are, for the rest of my life. Promise. Now come.' I held my hand out to him and pulled him up. We put our arms around each other's waists and matched our strides as we made our way back to the house.

As we reached the driveway, a car was winding its way up from the main gate. This time it had to be Aahana. I wanted to savour my last conversation with Akshar, I didn't want to meet Aahana. But the car was almost in front of us. She wasn't the only passenger, Dr Qureshi sat beside her.

Aahana got out of the car slowly. Akshar went up to her. She gave him a look that was so full that I felt she was communicating in a language only he could understand. Whatever Akshar might say I knew I came a very distant second. The words that had filled my heart just fifteen minutes back were ashes in my mouth now. How happy they had made me. How stupid was I?

Dr Qureshi was standing next to the car, waiting for something it seemed. But when no one seemed to intuit whatever it was he wanted, he suddenly spoke loudly. 'I'd like a few words with you, Akshar.'

Akshar and Aahana had reached the landing. He looked back at Dr Qureshi, nodded wearily and said, 'Come.'

Dr Qureshi rushed up the stairs. I walked up slowly behind him. Akshar turned to me. 'Will you go with her, Shalini?'

Aahana leaned against me. 'I don't know how I'll climb the stairs to the bedroom,' she muttered.

'Then stay downstairs? You can go up later.' I couldn't help but glance at her stomach, which had been so full and round the last time I saw her. Now it was distended but also bigger than I had expected. Like a collapsed drum.

'I'd rather go upstairs. We can go slowly.' I nodded. I assumed she was going to stay in Akshar's grand suite of rooms.

By the time we went upstairs, one slow step after another, Aahana was breathing heavily. Her eyes were sunken, she looked exhausted. She lay down on the large four-poster bed, and I put a quilt on her.

'Will you sit here with me, Shalini?' she asked softly.

Aahana patted the bed and I sat down. I remembered the little white bundle, I remembered the awful painting of that white bundle inside Aahana's stomach, under the earth. I thought of Akshar's mother, her silent, lifelong hatred of Aahana; that painting of Aahana, which was what? A prophecy, a dream, a wish? I thought of Dr Qureshi's cold slippery eyes and wondered how Aahana had managed to sleep in his bed all these months while being so desperately in love with Akshar. And now, finally, she was with Akshar, but what did they have left?

'Did you have a happy childhood, Shalini?' Aahana looked like a child herself, lying between the sheets, begging for a bedside story. I smiled.

'I don't know what that means, Aahana. At all.'

'Mine was a mess. Not devoid of love. There was love. But so much happened, all the time. Akshar … I just held on to Akshar.'

It was as if Akshar was the magic word. He entered the room as she said his name. I got up.

'Stay, Shalini,' he said. 'You are leaving soon as it is.'

'You are leaving?' Aahana asked. 'Can't we go away too, Akshar? We would get well, you would get well and we would be fine … away from here. This place, it isn't good.'

I agreed with her. This place, it was vile. But Akshar only frowned, displeased. 'This is where we belong, Aahana. Where would we go? You know the fires are spreading every day; it's only a matter of time, sweetheart. Just bear it all for a little while more.'

'What did Reyhan say?'

'Oh, that I will die soon and he will never take you back.' Akshar smiled.

'I can live with that.'

'I've spoken to your parents. I've explained my will to them.'

'Okay,' Aahana said listlessly. 'Please don't explain it to me now.'

'I guess I'll go and finish packing.' My words broke through their feeble conversation.

'If Aahana likes we can have dinner here,' Akshar looked at me. 'If she's tired, we can eat downstairs as usual.'

I went up the stairs slowly. I turned towards my room at the landing, assiduously avoiding Akshar's mother's chamber. My mind was writhing with all these half-formed notions. I really wanted to meet her, but something told me I must not. It was like she was the fire and if I looked at her now, I would be infected. I would burn.

Dinner was a quiet affair. None of us spoke much. I wandered off to my room without quite saying goodnight. The night wasn't over yet.

There was no electricity that evening. It was my first experience of a power cut in Akshar's home and a darkness so deep and velvety that I was loath to light the two candles that sat on the carved desk in my room, ready for exactly such an emergency. The matchbox next to the candles. Matches. It's best I avoided matches and matchboxes. My history with matchboxes and fire wasn't reassuring.

At once, the footsteps. Not soft and padded though. More like the quick tread of a person in a hurry. Then they slowed down. Right near my door. And there was an imperious knock.

I scrambled out of bed. It was Akshar. His grey-green eyes were flashing in the light of the torch he was holding when I opened the door.

'It's your last night,' he said, as if I might have forgotten. 'Can I come in?'

'Yes.' I let him inside and went back under my quilt. Akshar lit the two candles on the desk; the flames rose high and strong and I laughed aloud in a sudden flush of happiness and joy. Akshar didn't sit down, though I gestured at the chair near the window. He paced up and down instead. I watched him and the laughter of a moment ago died. A deep sadness welled up inside me and I knew it would never leave, like a little bit of me would always be stuck in this room after I left.

I sighed and got out of bed. The wind outside was cold and gusty, and my bedroom window was open. As I leaned forward to shut it, a movement below caught my eye.

'Akshar,' I said. 'Isn't that Aahana?'

Just a silhouette and difficult to identify in the dark, yet I was sure the figure was Aahana. I gestured to Akshar to come quickly but by the time he reached the window, she had gone around the bend and out of our line of vision.

'I think it was Aahana ...' Now that the figure had receded, I was unsure.

'I left her sleeping,' said Akshar but he didn't sound sure either. 'She's so weak and tired.'

'Yes, I might be mistaken.' I remembered how hard it had been for Aahana to climb the stairs in the afternoon. She couldn't have made the journey down and around the mansion in the middle of the night. 'But ...'

Akshar sighed. 'Let me go and check on her.'

'You want me to come with you?' I asked. I was filled with a curious misgiving and fear.

'Sure, come.'

'You go, I'll join you,' I said. I splashed some water on my face in the bathroom sink. I felt bone tired. I picked up one of the candles. It was slim and flimsy. The flames had become insubstantial. I wondered what would happen if I overturned the candles on to the desk. Would it catch fire? Chances were the candles would just blow out in the moisture-laden air, plunging the room in blackness rather than light.

I lit one matchstick, then another. I kept lighting and dropping the matchsticks, I loved the way the tips lit up and the way in which some caught fire, the tiny flame rising, and some went off, leaving a wisp of grey smoke. The floor was littered with flaming little matchsticks now.

I got lost in the corridor. I found myself standing in front of Akshar's mother's room. The silence was absolute. I knocked but didn't wait. I turned around and went down the passage, towards the staircase.

The main door to Akshar's suite of rooms was wide open. Akshar was at the door, about to leave the room, but he turned and shone his torch wordlessly at the bed, at the crumpled bedsheets with splashes of blood.

'I thought she was fast asleep at first. I tiptoed around the room like a fool. The sheets were bunched up as if she was under them. I was on my way back to your room but something made me come back and then I realized ...'

'But where is she? That blood ...' I said and Akshar seemed to come out of the semi-trance he was in. Then we were both running. We tore down the stairs and corridors and out of the main door. The cold wind hit us hard, and I could feel stray raindrops that were yet to turn into rainfall. I felt my head clear. It was good we were outside.

We turned the corner that would take us behind the mansion, to the tangled forest trails. We had been running for the last three or four minutes yet we hadn't spotted Aahana. How fast could she be walking in the condition she was in?

Akshar went past the gardener's cottage, to the steep incline that would lead down to the grassless patch where a tiny body was buried.

At first it seemed no human being was there. Just the trees bending and forming a canopy over the little grave, like a prayer. But then, as we stood there, I watched the earth near the grave shift. As my eyes adjusted to the dark I saw the outline of a body, crumpled, motionless, almost merging with the mud and plant life on the mossy ground. Akshar was running down the incline.

I stared at Aahana's prostrate form – she gave a sudden jerk and started thrashing around on the ground with freakish energy. The stillness of her body, just a few moments back, followed by this unnatural spasm of movement as she writhed on the ground. It was dreadful and mesmerizing. The wave of tremors ended and she crept forward on all fours with the crawling, spasmodic movement of a beast – towards the little white bundle that was lying on the ground. She had dug it out of the ground. Some perverted maternal instinct. It was disturbing, devastating.

Akshar was leaning over her but not touching her as she thrashed around, once more, before going limp. He gathered up her now-still body. I took slow steps towards them, knelt down on the ground and touched her forehead, which was clammy and cold. The earth next to us had been dug up in clumps. Aahana had exhumed the little grave frantically using her bare hands, with a fervour that had taken every last breath out of her body. She lay limp in Akshar's arms now.

Akshar ignored the bundle that had his dead boy inside it. What could he even do? Throw it back into the grave? I thought I saw the bundle move, as if the baby was thrashing around inside, exactly like his mother had been doing on the ground moments ago.

Akshar was hardly in the best of health himself but with some help from me he managed to stand up while carrying Aahana in his arms. She was frail and slim but still not small, and I didn't know what strength he summoned to stride up the mountain slope, slowly but without faltering. It was dark and the ground beneath our feet was rough and uneven. I turned around once but could no longer see the white bundle on the ground. Akshar didn't look back.

It took an age but we finally reached the mansion. After that last spasmodic shiver on the bare cold ground, Aahana hadn't moved at all. Her left arm hung lifeless. I wondered if she was breathing. In the distance, we could hear some shouting. Akshar muttered something which I didn't catch and we walked on till we turned the corner to the front of the building.

I had a sense of foreboding, as if I already knew what was coming. I kept glancing at Akshar, but his profile seemed carved from stone. His blank gaze was directed towards the driveway and at the people amassed there – Ravinder, Jai Singh and their families. One of the women was shrieking, and that seemed to confuse everyone further; they moved around as in a pantomime, helter-skelter, with no sense of direction or purpose. Someone spotted us and gave a shout, and for a split second everyone stood stock still. Ravinder and Jai Singh had been climbing the stairs to the main entrance but after the moment's pause, they ran towards us.

An unnatural haze lit up the air and there was an acrid smoky smell. It was all so familiar to me, like the return of an old, trusted friend. The words that Ravinder and Jai Singh were saying were high-pitched and distressed; they pointed upwards, and I saw that right above us the upper portions of the mansion were ablaze with flames and light and smoke.

I heard one of them say fire engine. But the fire was spreading fast, the strong flames demolishing windowpanes and creating havoc inside the rooms, in the corridors. It would soon reach my room and all that I'd carried for my four-day visit to Akshar would be gone – my laptop, my wallet, my driving licence. I wondered about the nurse, Akshar's mother and Sahil, whom I hadn't met in days.

Ravinder had called an ambulance too. Someone brought a garden chair for Akshar and he was seated with Aahana in his arms, still unconscious. In that uncanny light, staring unseeingly at the flames engulfing his family home, he didn't look like a living, breathing human being, more like a modern art installation that had been planted in front of this beautiful, sinister mansion that was gasping for breath.

A light seemed to have been switched on in Akshar's study on the ground floor. The top floor was ablaze now, bright orange-yellow flames erupting from every room and window. A light being flicked on in Akshar's study meant that his mother or the nurse or Sahil – or all three of them – must have made their way down and perhaps in a state of disorientation gone into the study instead of coming right out.

I looked at Akshar, but he was still staring blankly into the distance. I scratched the fleshy wound on my collarbone with my index fingernail, a childhood tic, till the pus started trickling down. I licked the finger and started sucking it, comforted like a toddler with a pacifier.

The crowd was milling at the main entrance, pointing at the study, running around, shouting. It didn't seem like only a light had been switched on in the study anymore. There were flames, there was fire and smoke. Was someone in the room – Akshar's mother, her nurse? I felt fear crawling on my skin. Was Adil there? I meant Sahil, of course, not Adil. Akshar's mother and I – two sides of the same coin. Poor Akshar, he was always doomed. Caught between all the women in his life, he hardly had a chance. I could feel that sick laughter inside me again, my left eyebrow twitching with the effort it took not to laugh.

I couldn't look at the flames in the study. I couldn't think of all those books, all those priceless pages of words and wisdom, slowly being reduced to ashes. Sentences destroyed, burnt and mangled. Reduced to a nothingness that would soon claim us, too. The fire wasn't being hasty, it was slowly creeping all around the globe, destroying in myriad ways that gave it pleasure. Disease, fire, floods, starvation. With a little human help. Always.

Around us, everyone was shouting and looking at the grand arched entranceway with its fluted columns. My blood turned to ice. I literally felt it happen, this cold slim thread of ice slithering under my skin. Smiling beatifically in a long, beige nightgown with ruffles and bows, Akshar's mother, tall, slim and regal, was standing at the top of the stairs and bowing and nodding as if accepting applause at a magnificent concert she had orchestrated.

It's difficult to explain how a smiling elderly woman with dementia, standing at the base of a mansion that was going up in flames, can strike terror in one's heart. But I knew everyone felt it. I knew fire, knew how it could make you go mad, make you forget. No one dared to move, to go towards her. Her streaming hair looked like it was on fire too, a dingy grey fire that shimmered and shook. Only Akshar seemed to not notice. He was still staring into a nullity, a void of his own, his grey-green eyes dead and beautiful, his long hair tucked behind his ears. An intricate Michelangelo figure from centuries ago, sculpted from the cold marble floors of his dying mansion.

Had my mother been scared of me, all those years back? Of the monster child she had birthed? When I had stood at the foot of her bed and stared at the flames? Over the years I had grudgingly come to accept that she had never quite given up on me. It was mostly a burden but sometimes it had been redemption – the knowledge that she didn't know how to stop hoping. Yet that child hasn't vanished, she continued to live inside me, in the nooks and crannies of my body, whispering to me, asking me to do things I mustn't.

Sahil came out of the flaming building in an unhurried, calm manner. There was a whoosh in the air, as if everyone had been holding their breaths till now – a collective forceful exhalation of relief at Sahil's arrival. A few people clapped. He put an arm around his mother and led her down the stairs, towards where we were. His eyes locked with mine and I suddenly knew that he knew. Not that it mattered. Those who knew, they always understood. I thought of Jugaad, his little body destroyed by fire. Sahil, the little boy who had been there that day.

The fire was still raging, spreading; the house was encased in shimmering heat and flame, ready to topple over and consume us all. Sparks were flying everywhere. Windowpanes, bricks, balcony railings – all crumbling, pieces flying through the air like broken firebirds, collapsing gracefully on the manicured pathways, the beautiful lawns. Yet none of us moved back. We stood staring, entranced.

That was when the singing began. It seemed to be coming from the direction of the main gate.

Two columns of women in their usual colourful attire, turbans and neckpieces, were coming up the driveway. More women than I'd seen in this town so far. They were chanting, some of them had musical instruments which tinkled and shivered, throwing joyous notes of music into the air. They were walking towards us, towards the mansion that was a giant fireball now.

It was then that I saw the prone figure in the middle of the two columns, held aloft by the women. The charred remains of a human but recognizable, not reduced to ashes. The terror that had been residing inside me for days (or was it years?) spread in waves through my whole body. My hand flew to my mouth, and then I was running. Running down the pathway towards the women. I knew who they were carrying. I didn't need to look closer to know. I flew through them, till I reached the body that seemed to be floating in midair.

The women bowed their heads, laid down their musical instruments and put the body down. The chanting continued. I was on my knees now, my face in my hands, my fingers wet from the tears, floods of tears that I didn't even know my eyes were capable of manufacturing. My first coherent thought was of Mukul's parents. How would they bear this? How would I tell them it was my fault?

I looked at Mukul's broken, burnt body, and my chest hurt, as if from the heat of the fire that had mauled him. He should have been at home, watering his plants, working on his laptop. Why was he here? Why did he come to get me? I looked around. I scanned the women. I stood up, took a few steps here and there. Baby steps. The faltering steps of a baby towards a parent. Steps that I'd never taken towards my mother. The child within me wanted my mother for the first time in my life. Where was she? I was frantic now.

One of the women who was standing in front of me put a hand on my shoulder. There was a world of wisdom in her eyes. She nodded, and I knew Ma was safe. She was letting me know Ma was safe. I felt relief flooding me. I sank down onto my knees again. I put my face against Mukul's charred body and wept.

EPILOGUE
The Remains

the woman in the room

The nurse had fallen fast asleep. She was exhausted. The woman had been so restless and agitated the last few nights. She would start pacing the room, throw things around, talk incessantly, shout sometimes. Her medicines did include tranquilizers but at times they made no difference and she would stay up all night, falling asleep as the moon paled and the mountains were backlit by the rising sun.

Tonight wasn't any different but the nurse had passed out on her couch near the window, despite the fact that Disha Gupta was still very much awake and pacing up and down. The nurse's open mouth and rather loud snores displeased Disha. She picked up the jug with the intention of pouring water on the nurse's head but the jug was heavy – she put it down.

The nurse stirred and opened her eyes only when the room got too hot. She saw Disha leaning over her. 'Are you feeling cold? I've lit a fire for you. Soon you will feel warm.' Disha said, happy the nurse was awake at last.

The nurse felt a burning sensation near her feet and a strange sort of heat by her side. She screamed as the fire hit the soles of her feet, and her brain froze. Disha quickly walked away to the other end of the room. The nurse forgot what she was supposed to do. Of course, she knew, she had the training, but her mind was blank. Her bed was alight – she jumped up and rushed towards the door, screaming. Some part of her brain was telling her not to run – the flames seemed to gather strength as she ran. Every nerve in her body tingled and the pain was unbearable as she reached the bedroom door. It took every ounce of her strength to pull open the heavy oak but the pain was too much, she slipped and fell with her feet stuck in the doorway.

The couch was a roaring conflagration, the fire was spreading across the room. Disha was fascinated. She walked to where the nurse lay, unconscious. The flames had reached the door but Disha didn't really notice or care. She stepped daintily over the nurse, floated out of the room and down the corridor. Her body did feel hot and sooty but that didn't matter. It was nice to walk around alone without the nurse trailing her all the time.

the woman who left

Mukul pulled up on the shoulder of the highway. He reached for the bottle of water on the backseat and held it out to Vasundhara.

'What happened?' he asked, his voice thick with anxiety.

Vasundhara had dozed off for a minute and woken up screaming. The way she had gripped the dashboard as if she was going to pass out had made him freeze. The car had screeched to a halt. Vasundhara took deep breaths to calm herself, to stop herself from collapsing.

'We're almost there?' she asked.

'Yes, we've entered the town,' Mukul answered in a soothing voice. 'Drink some water.'

But Vasundhara was staring at the windscreen. It was turning a strange shade of scarlet. Cracks were appearing.

'Mukul. Fire.' She opened the door on her side and tumbled out. She ran to the other side of the road, but he wasn't out yet. The door was jammed. Fire was licking at the door like in her dreams. Except this was for real, and Adil wasn't in the car. It was Mukul and she had to save him.

Vasundhara could see him grappling with the door, trying to get out. She banged on the glass and tried to force the door open. The smoke and flashes of heat were obscuring her vision. She screamed, she felt the flames on her. Mukul was inside the car, the heat was unbearable but she couldn't leave – she had to get him out.

She didn't see the women coming up to her. She was losing consciousness when cold hands yanked her away from the burning car – numerous hands. They held her until she stopped screaming, a group of women clad in colourful garments, their faces obscured by the flames.

The fire subsided as suddenly as it had raged. They took Mukul out of the car, his lifeless burnt body, and bore him away.

Vasundhara sat on the side of the road on the mountain, left with the nightmares that would never end.

the woman who was unafraid of fire

I don't know how much time passed before we heard the sirens of the fire engine and ambulance. Time crawling – one of those clichéd metaphors that anyone who has lived through a crisis of this nature will understand. Where was the nurse? I tried to unthink the question.

The details of the next few hours were murky. The fire being doused, the nurse's dead body brought out, Akshar's mother telling the police sweetly and politely that she had come down because the fire was too hot. No one wanted to cross-question an Alzheimer's patient. Just like all those years ago when no one had wanted to question me, a child. Little tongues of fire going through the middle of the mansion, splitting it into two. Some of us are always ready to self-destruct. Drawn to pain and disaster like moths to a flame. *Shama-parwana*. We die again and again.

Delhi was a still-life painting when Ma and I reached home. Empty streets like in old sepia photographs, shops with shutters permanently down, lost stray dogs worrying where the people of a bustling metropolis had disappeared.

Ma and I would never be able to build bridges the way other mothers and daughters did. The uneasy peace in the aftermath of all that had happened was as good as it could get. In spite of everything, or because of it, Ma's whole life had ultimately revolved around me. She would still drop everything to be by my side. I knew this, though I was incapable of reaching out for her. It was an imperfect love but there it was. It kept me safe.

Akshar came to stay with me after a few months, after Aahana had passed, after the world had calmed down, after Sahil and his mother had settled down in a small house overlooking the mountains. Akshar's eyes had bags under them, his thin lips bloodless and his skin so white and dry. Gaunt, with permanent dark circles, and carrying with him the smell of pines and mountain rain.

I reached out, took his right hand in my left and squeezed it. He didn't say anything but held on to my hand tightly as we watched the sun disappear behind distant buildings in a city that had now forgotten how to be frenetic, chaotic, mechanical. The earth was quiet for now, in a wary sort of way. The burnings belonged to the past, more or less. They were few and far between and there were strategies in place on how to manage them, like vaccines against diseases. But they could still push and nudge, ignite a madness within. And thus I would remain with the light and the flames nestled deep inside my very sinews and bones, I knew I would spend my life with them, trying to keep them quiet, making my peace with the embers that glowed and refused to die.

Akshar was quiet for the first few days. Then he started speaking. In fits and starts, out of the blue. In the kitchen while we were cooking, while hanging clothes from the washing machine out to dry. Akshar always joined me when I did any housework, though I knew now that he didn't lift a finger in his grand old mansion. Maybe it was the training from our boarding school days or when he had stayed by himself during his college days in the UK. Whatever it was, he didn't seem unfamiliar with housework, he chopped vegetables competently, dusted bookshelves, did the dishes. We were sitting on the balcony one night when Akshar reached out for me. I rested my head on his shoulder, and he pulled me closer and held me tight. His hands roamed, his lips sought out mine. I knew it wasn't me he wanted as much as the warmth of another person. I was alright with that. I didn't really have much to give these days either, except the physicality of a lust and longing that had always been there for Akshar to claim. For the next few days and nights we turned to each other, eagerly and often. It was as if our bodies had the power to restore, even if for a moment, what nothing else could.

I drifted into a dark, exhausted sleep night after night, a sleep in which this world and another fused together. I could see tiny flames licking at Akshar, splitting him into two, his ruptured flesh and bones melting into the ashes of his mansion, as it all levelled with the earth which had been there from the beginning of time, before the age of the fire, before we began.

Acknowledgements

Teesta Guha Sarkar, my brilliant friend and editor, for her perceptive and painstaking feedback, and Shreyoshee Bandyopadhyay, an editor par excellence and fellow lover of horror – Teesta and Shreyoshee's readings went a long way in improving the book. And to the rest of the team at Pan Macmillan India, especially Rajdeep Mukherjee, Vijay Sharma, Isha Banerji, Saburi Pandit, Divyanshi Dash and Pooja Sharma.

Sayantan Ghosh and our many conversations on horror which made me realize and own my love for this genre and for his recommendations of books and films that were crucial to my writing.

Diya Kar, who is always urging me to write and who read the terrible first draft of this novel and gently pushed me to make it better.

Sayoni Basu and Samit Tandon for the absurd, inane banter and occasional wisdom. Srija Umapathy, who has badgered me into loving her. To friends from my editorial and writing life who shape me in little and big ways as I go along – Payal Malhotra, Sanghamitra Biswas, Megha Mukherjee, Susan Dias, Paul Kumar,

Mridu Agarwal, Devika Rangachari, Nandita Basu, Megha Rao, Abhay Singh.

To my school and college friends, especially the BPG (won't spell this out and embarrass us all), and Chaitali and Sonika, with whom I've had more fallouts and reconciliations than with anyone else over the last many decades. To ALL my family (a special shout out to Neeta and Timtim who are conveniently located for food and gossip!), spread thickly like the mafia across Calcutta, Delhi, the US and Canada, especially my horde of moderately insane cousins. My brother, Abhrajit Mitra, who has always tiredly recalibrated his innate beliefs to accommodate his younger sister.

And finally, my daughters, Gayathri and Samhitha, and my husband, Sankar, whose first name is my last name, which is really quite irksome. No words for them. Just.